"Where are you taking me?" Abby asked from the passenger seat of the pickup.

He could tell that each word hurt her to speak. He would have brought the Suburban so she could lie down in the back but he hadn't known how badly she was hurt.

"To the hospital," he said.

"No!" She tried to sit up straight but cried out in pain and held her rib cage. "That's the first place he'll look for me."

"Abby, you need medical attention."

"Please."

He quickly relented. He couldn't let Wade near this woman, which meant no hospital. At least for now.

"I'll take you to the ranch and call our family doctor. But, Abby, if he says you have to go to the hospital—"

"Then I'll go." She lay back and closed her eyes. "I didn't want you involved."

"I've always been involved, because I've always loved you."

She said nothing. He could tell that she was in a lot of pain. It had him boiling inside. If he could find Wade right now...

DEAD RINGER

New York Times **Bestselling Author**

B.J. DANIELS

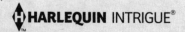

HARLEQUIN INTRIGUE®

This book is dedicated to JoAnn Hammond, who was one of the first in Whitewater to read one of my books :) So glad we got to know each other—and share a love for quilting and reading.

Recycling programs for this product may not exist in your area.

ISBN-13: 978-1-335-72119-8

Dead Ringer

Copyright © 2017 by Barbara Heinlein

Printed in U.S.A.

HARLEQUIN®
www.Harlequin.com

B.J. Daniels is a *New York Times* and *USA TODAY* bestselling author. She wrote her first book after a career as an award-winning newspaper journalist and author of thirty-seven published short stories. She lives in Montana with her husband, Parker, and three springer spaniels. When not writing, she quilts, boats and plays tennis. Contact her at bjdaniels.com, on Facebook or on Twitter, @bjdanielsauthor.

Books by B.J. Daniels

Harlequin Intrigue

Whitehorse, Montana: The McGraw Kidnapping

Dark Horse
Rough Rider
Dead Ringer

Whitehorse, Montana

Secret of Deadman's Coulee
The New Deputy in Town
The Mystery Man of Whitehorse
Classified Christmas
Matchmaking with a Mission
Second Chance Cowboy
Montana Royalty
Shotgun Bride

Visit the Author Profile page at Harlequin.com.

CAST OF CHARACTERS

Ledger McGraw—Nothing can keep him from helping the woman he loves—even a marriage license.

Abby Pierce—She promised to love her husband until death. But if she stays, she is a dead woman.

Travers McGraw—He has believed for twenty-five years that his kidnapped babies are alive and will somehow find their way home.

Wade Pierce—He got Abby, but he had to cheat to do it and it eats at him. But he'd kill her before he'd let anyone else have her.

Huck Pierce—When it comes to the McGraws, he has his reasons for hating them.

Jim Waters—The attorney is hanging on to his job by a thread, but then he finds one of the kidnapped children.

Vance Elliot—The good-looking adopted saddle tramp has proof that he's Oakley McGraw, the missing twin.

Tough Crandall—With his green eyes and dark hair, he throws a monkey wrench into well-laid plans.

Chapter One

Abby Pierce opened her eyes and quickly closed them against the bright sunlight. She hurt all over. As she tried to sit up, a hand gently pushed on her shoulder to keep her flat on the bed.

"Don't sit up too fast," her husband said. "You're okay. You're in the hospital. You took a nasty fall."

Fall? Hospital? Her mouth felt dry as dust. She licked her lips. "Can you close the drapes?"

"Sure," Wade said and hurried over to the window.

She listened as he drew the drapes together and felt the room darken before she opened her eyes all the way.

The first thing she saw was her husband silhouetted against the curtains. He was a big imposing man with a boyish face and a blond crew cut. He was wearing his sheriff's deputy uniform, she noted as he moved back to the bed to take her hand.

She'd known Wade for years. She'd married him three years ago. That was why when she saw the sheepish look in his brown eyes, she knew at once that he was hiding something.

Abby frowned. "What was I doing that I fell?"

"You don't remember?" He cleared his throat, shifting on his feet. "You asked me to bring up some canning jars from the garage? I'm so sorry I didn't. If I had you wouldn't have been on that ladder…" He looked at her as if expecting… Expecting what?

"Canning jars?" she repeated and touched her bandaged temple. "I hit my head?"

He nodded, and taking her hand, he squeezed it a little too hard. "I'm so sorry, Abby." He sounded close to tears.

"It's not your fault," she said automatically, but couldn't help but wonder if there was more to the story. There often was with Wade and his family. She frowned, trying to understand why she would have wanted canning jars and saying as much.

"You said something about putting up peach jam."

"Really? I wonder where I planned to get peaches this time of year."

He said nothing, avoiding her gaze. All the other times she'd seen him like this it had been after he'd hurt her. It had started a year into their marriage and begun with angry accusations that led to him grabbing her, shaking her, pushing her and even slapping her.

Each time he'd stopped before it had gone too far. Each time he'd been horrified by what he'd done. He'd cried in her arms, begging her to forgive him, telling her that he couldn't live without her, saying he would kill himself if she ever left him. And then promising he'd never do it again.

She touched her bandaged head with her free hand. The movement brought a groan out of her as she realized her ribs were either bruised or maybe even broken. Looking down, she saw the bruises on her wrists and knew he was lying. Had he pushed her this time?

"Why can't I remember what happened?" she asked.

"You can't remember *anything*?" He sounded hopeful, fueling her worst fears that one of these days he would go too far and kill her. Wasn't that what her former boyfriend kept telling her? She pushed the thought of Ledger McGraw away as she often had to do. He didn't understand that she'd promised to love, honor and obey when she'd married Wade— even through the rough spots. And this she feared was one of them.

At the sound of someone entering the room, they both turned to see the doctor come in.

"How are we doing?" he asked as he moved to the foot of her bed to look at her chart. He glanced at Wade, then quickly looked away. Wade let go of her hand and moved to the window to part the drapes and peer out.

Abby closed her eyes at the shaft of sunlight he let in. "My head hurts," she told the doctor.

"I would imagine it does. When your husband brought you in, you were in and out of consciousness."

Wade had brought her in? He didn't call an ambulance?

"Also I can't seem to remember what happened," she added and, out of the corner of her eye, saw her husband glance back at her.

The doctor nodded. "Very common in your type of head injury."

"Will she get her memory back?" Wade asked from the window, sounding worried that she would.

"Possibly. Often not. I'm going to prescribe something for your headache. Your ribs are badly bruised and you have some other abrasions. I'd like to keep you overnight."

"Is that really necessary?" Wade asked, letting the drapes drop back into place.

"With a concussion, it's best," the doctor said

without looking at him. "Don't worry. We'll take good care of her."

"We can talk about it," Wade said. "But I think she'd be more comfortable in her own home. Isn't that right, Abby?"

"On this, I think I know best," the doctor interrupted.

But she could see that Wade *was* worried. He apparently wanted to get her out of here and quickly. What was he worried about? That she would remember what happened?

If only she could. Unfortunately, the harder she tried, the more she couldn't. The past twenty-four hours were blank, leaving her with the terrifying feeling that her life depended on her remembering.

Chapter Two

When the phone rang at the Sundown Stallion Station late that afternoon, Ledger McGraw took the call since both his brothers were gone from the ranch and his father was resting upstairs. They had been forced to get an unlisted number after all the media coverage. After twenty-five years, there'd finally been a break in the McGraw twins kidnapping case.

"I need to talk to Travers," Jim Waters said without preamble. "Tell him it is of utmost importance."

Ledger groaned inwardly since he knew his father had almost fired the family attorney recently. "He's resting." Travers McGraw, sixty, had suffered a heart attack a few months ago. He hadn't been well before that. At the time, they hadn't known what was making him so sick. His family had assumed it was the stress of losing his two youngest children to kidnappers twenty-five years before and his determination to find them. His father was convinced that they were still alive.

"Do you really think I would be calling if it wasn't urgent?" Waters demanded. The fiftysomething attorney had been like one of the family almost from the beginning—until a few months ago, when he and Travers had gotten into a disagreement.

"Jim, if this is about legal business—"

The attorney swore. "It's about the kidnapping. You might recall that we originally used my number to screen the calls about the twins. Well, I am apparently still on the list. I was contacted." He paused, no doubt for effect. "I have reason to believe that Oakley has been found."

"Found?" Ledger asked, his heart in his throat. The twenty-fifth anniversary of the crime had come and gone, but after their father had hired a true-crime writer to investigate and write a book about it, new evidence had turned up.

That new evidence had led them all to believe that his father's gut instinct was right. The twins were alive—and probably adopted out to good families, though illegally. The McGraw twins had been just six months old when they were stolen from their cribs. The ransom money had never been spent and had only recently turned up—with the body of one of the kidnappers. That left whoever had helped him take the babies still at large.

Ledger was thankful that he'd been the one to answer the phone. His father didn't need this kind of aggravation. "All those calls are now being vetted by the sheriff's department. I suggest you have this person contact Sheriff McCall Crawford. If she thinks—"

"He has the stuffed toy horse," Waters interrupted. "I've seen it. It's Oakley's."

Ledger felt a shock wave move through him. The stuffed toy horse was a critical piece of information that hadn't originally been released to the public. Was it possible his little brother really had turned up? "Are you sure? There must have been thousands of those produced."

"Not with a certain ribbon tied around its neck." The information about the missing stuffed animal was recently released to the press—sans anything about the ribbon and other things about this specific toy. "Oakley's stuffed horse had a black saddle and a small tear where the stitching had been missed when it was made, right?"

He nodded to himself before saying, *"You say you've seen it?"* It was that small detail that no one would know unless they had Oakley's horse, which had been taken out of his crib along with him that night twenty-five years ago. "Have you met him?"

"I have. He sent me a photo of the stuffed horse. When I recognized it, I drove down to talk to him. Ledger, he swears he's had the stuffed horse since he was a baby."

Letting out a breath, he dropped into a nearby chair. A few months ago they'd learned that the babies might have been left with a member of the Whitehorse Sewing Circle, a group of older women quilters who placed unwanted babies with families desperate for a child. The quilting group had been operating illegally for decades.

Not that the twins had been unwanted. But the kidnapper had been led to believe that was the case. The hope had been that the babies had been well taken care of and that they were still alive, the theory being that they had no idea they'd been kidnapped. His father had made the decision to release more information about what had been taken along with the babies in the hopes that the twins would see it and come forward.

And now it had happened.

"What's his name?" Ledger asked as he gave himself a few minutes to take this all in and decide what to do. He didn't want to bother his father with this unless he was sure it wasn't a hoax.

"He goes by Vance Elliot. He's in Whitehorse. He wants to see your father."

"ABBY DOESN'T REMEMBER ANYTHING," Wade said as he walked past his father straight into the kitchen to pull a can of beer out of the refrigerator.

He popped the top, took a long swig and turned to find his father standing in the kitchen doorway frowning at him.

"I'll pay you back," he said, thinking the look was because he was drinking his old man's beer.

"What do you mean she doesn't remember *anything*?"

"I was skeptical at first, too," he said, drawing out a chair and spinning it around so he could straddle it backward at the table. "But when I told her she fell off a ladder in the garage, she bought it. She couldn't remember why she would have been on a ladder in the garage. I told her she was going to get jars to put up some peach jam."

Huck Pierce wagged his head. "Where in the hell would she get peaches this time of year?"

"How should I know? It doesn't matter. She's not putting up any jam. Nor is she saying a word about anything."

"You are one lucky son of a gun, then," Huck said.

"Don't I know it? So everything is cool, right?"

"Seems so. But I want you to stay by your wife's side. Keep everything as normal as possible. Stick to your story. If she starts to remember…" He shrugged. "We'll deal with it if we have to."

Wade downed the rest of his beer, needing it even though he was technically on duty at the sheriff's department. He didn't want his father to see how relieved he was. Or how worried about what would happen if Abby remembered what had really happened to her.

"Great, so I get to hang out at the hospital until my shift starts. That place gives me the creeps."

"You're the one who screwed everything up. You knew what was at stake," his father said angrily.

"Exactly." Wade knew he couldn't win in an argument with his father, but that didn't stop him. "So what was I supposed to do when she confronted me? I tried to reason with her, but you know how she is. She was threatening to call the sheriff. Or go running to her old boyfriend Ledger McGraw. I didn't have a choice but to try to stop her."

"What you're saying is that you can't handle your wife. At least you don't have some snot-nosed mouthy kid like I did."

"Yeah, thanks," he said, crushing the beer can in his hand. "I've heard all about how hard it was raising me." He reached in the refrigerator for another beer, knowing he shouldn't, but needing the buzz badly.

Before he could pull one out, his father slammed the refrigerator door, almost crushing his hand. "Get some gum. You can't have beer on your breath when you go back to the hospital, let alone come to work later. Remember, you're the worried husband, you damned fool."

LEDGER HAD JUST hung up with the attorney when he got the call from his friend who worked at the hospital.

"I shouldn't be calling you, but thought you'd want to know," she said, keeping her voice down. "Abby was brought in."

"That son of a—"

"He swears she fell off a ladder."

"Sure she did. I'll be right there. Is Wade—"

"He just left to go work his shift at the sheriff's department. The doctor is keeping Abby overnight."

"Is she okay?"

"She's pretty beat up, but she's going to be fine."

He breathed a sigh of relief as he hung up. When it rained it poured, he thought as he saw his father coming down the stairs toward him. Travers McGraw was still weak from his heart attack, but it was the systematic poisoning that had really almost killed him. Fortunately, his would-be killer was now behind bars awaiting trial.

But realizing that his second wife was trying to kill him had taken a toll on his father. It was bad enough that his first wife, Ledger's mother, was in a mental hospital. After the twins were kidnapped, Marianne McGraw had a complete breakdown. For twenty-five years, it was believed that she and the ranch's horse trainer, Nate Corwin, had been behind the kidnapping. Only recently had Nate's name been cleared.

"I heard the phone," Travers said now. He'd recovered, but was still weak. He'd lost too much weight. It would be a while until he was his old self. If ever.

That was why Ledger wasn't sure how his father would take the news Waters had called with earlier—especially if it led to yet another disappointment. And yet Ledger couldn't keep the attorney's call from him. If there was even the slightest chance that this Vance Elliot was Oakley…

"You should sit down."

His father didn't argue as he moved to a chair and sat. He seemed to brace himself. "What's happened?"

"Jim Waters called."

Travers began to shake his head. "Now what?"

"He's still apparently the contact person for the family on some of the old publicity," Ledger said.

His father knew at once. "Oakley or Jesse Rose?"

"Oakley. Jim says the young man has the stuffed horse that was taken along with Oakley from his crib the night of the kidnapping. He says he's seen the toy and that it is definitely Oakley's."

His father's eyes filled to overflowing. "Thank God. I knew they were alive. I've…felt it all these years."

"Dad, this Vance Elliot might not be Oakley. We have to keep that in mind."

"He has Oakley's stuffed horse."

"But we don't know how he got it or if it was with Oakley when he was given to the woman at the Whitehorse Sewing Circle," Ledger reminded him.

"When can I see him?" his father asked, getting to his feet.

"He's in town. Waters wants to bring him over this evening. I said it would be fine. I hope that was all right. If it goes well, I thought you might want him to stay for dinner. I can tell the cook." Their cook for as far back as Ledger could remember had recently been killed. They'd been through several cooks since then. He couldn't remember the name of the latest one right now and felt bad about it. "Let's just keep our fingers crossed that it really is Oakley."

His father smiled and stepped closer to him to place a hand on his shoulder. "I am so blessed to have such good sons. Speaking of sons, where are Cull and Boone?"

"Cull and Nikki are checking into some of the adoptions through the Whitehorse Sewing Circle." Nikki St. James was the crime writer who'd helped unlock some of the kidnapping mystery—and stolen Cull's heart.

"I doubt the twins' adoptions were recorded anywhere, and with the Cavanaugh woman dying not long after the twins were kidnapped... You haven't heard anything yet?"

Ledger shook his head. "They said that clues to what happened to some of the babies were found stitched on their baby blankets. But the twins wouldn't have quilted blankets made for them because of the circumstances." Pearl Cavanaugh had been led to believe that the twins were in danger, so she would have made very private adoptions for Oakley and Jesse Rose.

"And Boone?"

"He went to check on that horse you were interested in, remember?"

Travers nodded, frowning. Loss of memory was part of the effects of arsenic poisoning. "Maybe I'll just rest until dinner."

Ledger watched his father go back up the stairs before he headed for his pickup and the hospital.

"YOU SHOULDN'T BE HERE," Abby said the moment she opened her eyes and saw Ledger standing at the end of her bed. Her heart had taken off like a wild stallion at just the sight of him. It always did. "Wade could come back at any time."

Ledger had been her first love. He'd left an ache in her that she'd hoped would fade, if not eventually go away. But if anything, the ache had grown stronger. He'd broken her heart. It was why she'd married Wade. But ever since then, he'd been coming around, confusing her and making being married to Wade even harder. He seemed to think he had to save her from her husband.

It didn't help that Ledger McGraw had breakfast on the mornings that she waitressed at the White-horse Café. She'd done nothing to encourage him, although Wade didn't believe that.

Fortunately, Wade had only come down to the restaurant one time threatening to kill Ledger. Ledger had called him on it, saying they should step outside and finish it like men.

"Or do you only hit defenseless women?" Ledger had demanded of him.

Wade lost his temper and charged him. Ledger

had stepped aside, nailing Wade on the back of his neck as he lumbered past. Abby had screamed as Wade slammed headfirst into a table. He'd missed two weeks' work because of his neck and threatened to sue the McGraws for his pain and suffering.

She knew his neck wasn't hurt that badly, but he'd milked it, telling everyone that Ledger had blindsided him.

Wade's jealousy had gotten worse after that. Even when she'd reminded him again and again, "But you're the one I married."

"Only because you couldn't have McGraw," he would snap.

Ledger's name was never spoken in their house—at least not by her. Wade blamed him for everything that was wrong with their marriage—especially the fact that she hadn't given him a son.

They'd tried to get pregnant when they'd first married. Since he'd joined the sheriff's department and changed, she'd gone back on the pill in secret, hating that she kept it from him. She told herself that when things changed back to what she thought of as normal, she would go off the pill again.

Now she couldn't even remember what normal was anymore.

Ledger took a step toward her. He looked both

worried and furious. It scared her that he and Wade might get into another altercation because of her.

"I didn't come until I was sure Wade wasn't here," Ledger said as he came around the side of her bed. "When I heard, I had to see you. *You fell off a ladder?*"

She nodded even though it hurt her head to do so. "Clumsy." She avoided his gaze because she knew he wouldn't believe it any more than she did.

"What were you doing on a ladder?"

"Apparently I was getting down some canning jars to put up peach jam."

Ledger looked at her hard. "*Apparently?* You don't remember?"

"I seem to have lost the past twenty-four hours."

"Oh, Abby."

She could tell that he thought she was covering for Wade. It almost made her laugh since she'd covered for him enough times. This just wasn't one of them. She really couldn't remember *anything*.

Ledger started to reach for her hand, but must have thought better of it. She tucked her hand under the sheet so he wouldn't be tempted again. She couldn't have Wade walking in on that. It would be bad enough Ledger just being here.

"It was a stupid accident. I probably wasn't paying attention. I'm fine."

He made a face that said he didn't believe it as he reached out to brush the dark hair back from her forehead.

She flinched at his touch and he quickly pulled back his fingers. "Sorry," he said quickly. "Did I hurt you?"

Abby shook her head. His touch had always sparked desire in her, but she wasn't about to admit that. "My head hurts, is all."

She looked toward the door, worried that Wade might stop by. When he'd left, she could tell that he hadn't liked leaving her. Even though he was supposed to be on duty as a sheriff's deputy, he could swing by if he was worried about her, especially since he was determined to take her home.

Ledger followed her gaze as if he knew what was making her so nervous. "I'll go," he said. "But if I find out that Wade had anything to do with this—"

"I fell off a ladder." She knew it was a lie, and from the look in Ledger's eyes, he did, too. But she had to at least try to convince him that Wade was innocent. This time. "That's all it was."

She met his gaze and felt her heart break as it always did. "Thank you for stopping by," she said even though there was so much more she wanted to say to him. But she was Wade's *wife*. As her mother always said, she'd made her bed and now she had to lie in it for better or worse.

Not that her mother didn't always remind her that Ledger hadn't wanted her.

"I'm here for you, Abby. If you ever need me…"

She felt tears burn her eyes. If only that had been true before she'd married Wade. "I can't." Her heart broke as she dragged her gaze away from his.

As if resigned, she watched out of the corner of her eye as he put on his Stetson, tipped it to her and walked out.

ATTORNEY JIM WATERS looked at the young man sitting in the passenger seat of his car as he drove toward the ranch later that evening. Vance Elliot. Here was Waters's ticket back into the McGraws' good graces.

He'd bet on the wrong horse, so to speak. Travers's second wife, Patricia McGraw, had been a good bet at the time. Pretty, sexy, almost twenty years younger than her husband. She'd convinced him Travers wasn't himself. That she needed a man she could count on. She'd let him believe that he might be living in that big house soon with her because Travers had some incurable ailment that only she and Travers knew about.

He'd bought into it hook, line and sinker. And why wouldn't he? Travers had been sick—anyone could see that. Also the man had seemed distracted, often forgetful and vague as if he was losing his mind. He'd been convinced that Travers wasn't long with this world and that Patricia would be taking over the ranch.

Little did he know that she was *poisoning* her husband.

As it turned out, Patricia was now behind bars awaiting trial. Since he had stupidly sided with her, things had gone downhill from there. He was hanging on to his job with Travers by the skin of his teeth.

But this was going to make it all right again, he told himself. He couldn't let a paycheck like McGraw get away. His retainer alone would keep him nicely for years to come. He just needed to get Travers's trust back. He saw a lot more legal work on the horizon for the McGraws. If this young man was Oakley, he would be back in the McGraw fold.

His cell phone rang. Patricia McGraw again. Travers's young wife wouldn't quit calling even though he'd told her he wasn't going to help her, let alone defend her.

Nor did he need to hear any of her threats. Fortunately, no one believed anything she said. Since Travers McGraw was idolized in this county, people saw her as the gold digger who'd married him—and then systematically tried to kill him. She got no sympathy. In fact, he doubted she could get even a fair trial.

"I'm innocent, you bastard," she'd screamed the last time he'd taken her call. "You did this. You framed me for this. Once I tell the sheriff—"

He'd laughed. "Like anyone will believe you."

"I'll take you down with me!"

He'd hung up and the next time his phone had rung it had been Vance Elliot.

Waters slowed to turn into the lane that led up to the main house. He shot the man next to him a glance. Vance looked more like a teenager than a twenty-five-year-old.

The man who might be Oakley stared at the house, a little openmouthed. Waters remembered the first time he'd driven out here and seen it. The house was impressive. So were the miles of white wooden fence, the expensive quarter horses in the pasture and the section after section of land that ran to the Little Rockies.

He couldn't imagine what it would be like to learn that he was part of this even at his age—let alone twenty-five. If Vance Elliot really was the long-ago kidnapped McGraw twin, then he was one lucky son of a gun.

"You all right?" he asked Vance as they drove toward the house.

The man nodded. Waters tried to read him. He had to be scared to face Travers McGraw, not to mention his three older sons. But he didn't look it. He looked determined.

Waters felt his stomach roil. This had better be real. If this wasn't Oakley McGraw he was bringing to Travers...

He didn't want to think about how badly this could go for him.

Chapter Three

Sheriff McCall Crawford happened to be standing at the window as Huck and Wade Pierce had come into work. Wade looked wrung out. She'd heard that his wife was in the hospital with a concussion after falling off a ladder.

McCall watched the two men. She'd inherited Huck when she'd become sheriff. Before that, she'd worked with him as a deputy. He'd made it clear that he thought a woman's place was in the home and not carrying a badge and gun. Huck hadn't been any more impressed when he'd been passed over and she'd become sheriff.

He was a good old boy, the kind who smiled in your face and stabbed you in the back the first chance he got. She didn't trust him, but she couldn't fire him without cause. So far, he'd done nothing to warrant it, but she kept her eye on him—and his son, Wade. The minute she caught him stepping over the line, he was gone. As for his son… She'd had hopes for him when he'd hired on, seeing something in him that could go a different way than his father. Lately, though…

Both looked up as if sensing her watching them from the window. She raised her coffee mug in a salute to them. Their expressions turned solemn as they entered the building.

Neither man was stupid. Both were hanging on by a thread, and if the rumors about Wade mistreating his wife could ever be proved, he would be gone soon. But in a small community like this, it was hard to prove there was a problem unless the wife came forward. So far, Abby hadn't. But now she was in the hospital after allegedly falling off a ladder. Maybe this would be the straw that broke the camel's back.

McCall's cell phone rang. She stepped to her desk and picked up, seeing that it was her grandmother. It felt strange having a relationship with her after all those years of never even laying eyes on the woman.

"Good evening," she said into the phone.

"What are you still doing at work this late?" Pepper demanded.

"I was just about to leave," McCall said. The day had gotten away from her after she dropped her daughter off at day care and came in to deal with all the paperwork that tended to stack up on her desk.

Most of the time, she and Luke could work out a schedule where one—if not both of them—was home with Tracey.

But several days a week, her daughter had to go to a day care near the sheriff's office in downtown Whitehorse. McCall had checked it out carefully and found no problems with the two women who ran it. Tracey seemed to love going because she was around other children. For a working mother, it was the best McCall could do.

"So is there any truth to it?" her grandmother demanded in her no-nonsense normal tone of voice. "Has one of the McGraw twins been found?"

The question took McCall by surprise. For twenty-five years there had been no news on the fraternal twins who'd been kidnapped. Then a few months ago a true-crime writer had shown up at the Mc-Graw ranch and all hell had broken loose. While some pieces of the puzzle had been found, the twins hadn't been yet.

Now was it possible one of them had been located?

"I heard it's the boy, Oakley," her grandmother was saying. "Apparently your theory about who might have adopted out the children was correct. It was the Whitehorse Sewing Circle. That bunch of old hens. You should arrest them all." Most of the women involved in the illegal kidnappings were dead now. "On top of that, that crazy daughter of Arlene Evans almost escaped from the loony bin last night."

McCall hadn't heard about that, either. It amazed her that Pepper often knew what was going on in town before the sheriff did—even though the Winchester Ranch was miles south of Whitehorse.

"Thank you for all the information. Is that it? Or was the bank robbed?"

Pepper laughed. "You should hire me since I know more of what is going on than you do." It was an old refrain, one McCall almost enjoyed. Almost.

"Well, let me know when you find out something worth hearing about," Pepper said. "I'm having lunch with the rest of your family tomorrow. Maybe sometime you can come out." With that, her grandmother was gone, leaving McCall to smile before she dialed Travers McGraw's number.

VANCE ELLIOT WATCHED the landscape blur past and wiped his sweaty palms on his jeans.

"You all right?" the attorney asked from behind the wheel of the SUV. The fiftysomething man wore a dark suit, reminding Vance of an undertaker. No one wore a suit like that, not around these parts, anyway. So Jim Waters must be some highfalutin lawyer who made a lot of money. But then, he worked for Travers McGraw, Vance thought as he saw the huge ranch ahead. Travers McGraw probably paid him well.

"I'm a little nervous," he admitted in answer to the lawyer's question. He was about to come face-to-face with Travers McGraw and his three sons. He'd heard enough about them to be anxious. Plus, the attorney had already warned him.

"They aren't going to believe you, but don't let that rattle you," Waters said. "They've had a lot of people pretend to be the missing twins, so naturally they're going to be suspicious. But having the stuffed horse will help. Then there is the DNA test. You're ready for that, right?"

Right. That alone scared the daylights out of him, but he simply nodded to the attorney's question.

He watched the ranch house come into view. He couldn't imagine growing up on a place like this. Couldn't imagine having that much land or that much money. Nor could he deny the appeal of being a McGraw with all the privileges that came with it.

He knew he was getting ahead of himself. There were a lot of hoops he had to jump through before they would accept that he was Oakley, the missing twin. But at least he could admire the house until then. It was huge with several wings that trailed off from the two-story center.

He'd heard stories about lavish parties where senators and even the governor had attended. That was before the twins were kidnapped, though, before the first Mrs. McGraw went to the loony bin and the second one went to jail.

But the house and grounds were still beautiful, and the horses… A half dozen raced through a nearby pasture as beautiful as any horseflesh he'd ever seen. Horses were in his blood, he thought with a silent laugh. And as Waters turned into the long lane leading to the house, he thought maybe horses were in his future.

"There is nothing to be afraid of," the attorney said. "Just tell them what you told me."

"I will." He swallowed the lump in his throat. Just stick to the story. The attorney had believed him. So Travers McGraw should, too, right? The stuffed horse had opened the door. The DNA test would cinch it.

As Waters brought the SUV to a stop in front of the house, Vance picked up the paper bag next to him and held it like a suit of armor to his chest.

"Try to relax," the attorney said. "You look like you're going to jump out of your skin."

He took a deep breath and thought of his run-ins with the law as a horse thief. He'd talked his way out of those. He could handle this.

Think about the payoff, he reminded himself. This place could be his one day.

"DAD, I DON'T want you getting upset," Boone Mc-Graw said as they waited in Travers's office. "You know what the doctor said."

"I had a heart attack," his father said impatiently. "Given the state of my health and why it was so bad, I'm fine now. Even the doctor is amazed how quickly I've bounced back."

Ledger stood by the office fireplace, as anxious as the rest of his family. They all knew that their father had bounced back because even before this phone call, Travers McGraw was determined the twins were alive and that he would see them again.

And now, after releasing more information to the press, maybe one of the twins had come forward. Ledger couldn't help being skeptical. They'd been here before. Except this time, this one had Oakley's stuffed horse, which had been in his crib the night he was kidnapped. Would his father finally be able to find some peace?

Or, after twenty-five years, had too much time passed? Oakley would be a grown man, no longer that cute six-month-old baby who'd been stolen. He would have lived a good portion of his life as someone else, with other parents. He would have his own life and the McGraws would all be strangers to him.

Ledger feared this wasn't going to be the homecoming his father was hoping for as he heard a vehicle pull up out front. He looked from his father to his brother and then went to answer the door. Better him than Boone, who already looked as if he could chew nails. It was going to take a lot to convince Boone that whoever was headed for the door was the lost twin.

Unable to wait for a knock, Ledger opened the door. Attorney Jim Waters and the young man, who might or might not be his brother, were at the bottom of the porch steps. His gaze went right to the young man, who looked dressed in all new clothing from the button-down shirt to the jeans and Western boots. He was tall, broad-shouldered and slim hipped like all the McGraw men.

At the sound of the front door opening, Vance Elliot looked up, his thick dark hair falling over his forehead. Ledger saw the blue eyes and felt a shiver.

This might really be his brother.

"Vance Elliot, this is Ledger McGraw," Waters said by introduction.

"Please, come in," he said, unable to take his eyes off the young man. "My father and brother are in his office."

LEDGER LED THE two men into his father's office and closed the door. The new cook, a woman by the name of Louise, he'd made a point of learning, was in the kitchen making dinner. Cull and Nikki should be back soon. Unless they decided to stay in Whitehorse and go out to dinner. He still couldn't believe how hard his brother had fallen for the true-crime writer.

"Please sit down," Travers said, getting to his feet to shake hands with Vance. He waited until everyone was sitting before he asked, "So you think you might be my son Oakley. Why don't you start by telling us something about you?"

Vance shifted in his chair. He held a large paper bag on his lap, the top turned under. Ledger assumed the stuffed toy horse was inside. He would have thought his father would want to see it right away.

"I don't know exactly where to begin. I was raised in Bear Creek, south of Billings, on a small farm. My parents told me when I was about five that I was adopted."

"Did you have other siblings?" Travers asked.

Vance shook his head. "Just me." He shrugged. "I had a fine childhood. We didn't have much but it was enough. I went to college in Billings for a while before getting a job on a ranch outside of Belfry. That's about it."

"And how did you become aware that you might be one of the missing McGraw twins?" his father asked.

"I heard about it on television. When they mentioned the small stuffed horse and showed a photo of what it might look like, I couldn't believe it. I'd had one just like it as far back as I could remember."

"Is that what's in the bag?" Boone asked.

Vance nodded and stood to place the bag on the desk in front of Travers. He took a step back, bumped into the chair and sat again.

The room had gone deathly quiet. Ledger could hear nothing but his own heart pounding as his father pulled the bag closer, unfolded the top and looked inside.

A small gasp escaped his father's lips as he pulled the toy stuffed horse from the bag. Ledger saw the worn blue ribbon around the horse's neck and swung his gaze to Vance. If he was telling the truth, then this man was Oakley, all grown up.

WATERS COULDN'T HELP the self-satisfied feeling he had when he saw Travers McGraw's expression. He'd felt the same way when he'd seen the toy stuffed horse. It was Oakley's; there was no doubt about that.

Of course, this wouldn't be a done deal until

after the DNA tests were run, but he was on the home stretch.

"Would the two of you like to stay for dinner?" Travers asked, putting the toy back into the sack and rising to his feet. "I'd like to hear more about your childhood, Vance." It was clear he was fighting calling the young man by that name.

He'd also seen Travers's face when the two of them had walked into the office. The horse rancher had looked shocked by how much the young man resembled Travers's own sons.

Waters looked to Vance before he said, "We'd love to stay for dinner. If you're sure it isn't an inconvenience." He thought of the years he'd sat at the big dining room table and eaten under this roof. If this went the way he expected it to, he'd be a regular guest again.

"Wonderful," Travers said as he came around his desk. Putting an arm around Vance, he steered him toward the dining room at the back of the house. "Where are you staying?"

Vance cleared his voice. "I spent last night at a motel in town."

"You can stay here on the ranch if you'd like," Travers said. "I don't want to pressure you. Give it some thought. We can discuss it after dinner."

Waters smiled to himself. This couldn't have gone

any better. Vance was in—at least until the DNA test. But if he passed that...

His cell phone vibrated in his pocket. He checked caller ID. Patricia, the soon-to-be former wife of Travers McGraw. He was sure his boss would ask him to handle the divorce. It would be his pleasure.

Chapter Four

Abby was dressed and sitting in the wheelchair waiting when her husband came into her hospital room the next afternoon. She felt fine, except for a headache and no memory of what had happened to her. But hospital policy required her to be "driven" down to the exit by wheelchair after her doctor came in.

Wade stopped in the doorway. She gave him a smile to reassure him that she was all right. He'd been so worried. She'd never seen him like that before.

He tried to smile back, but his expression crumbled. He burst into tears, dropping to his knees in front of her wheelchair.

"Oh, babe, I'm so sorry."

"Wade, this wasn't your fault. You have to quit blaming yourself," Abby said, wishing it was true, as he squeezed her hand with what felt like desperation.

"I just don't know what I would do if I lost you,"

he was saying. "When I thought you were dead…
Abby, I love you so much. Sometimes I do stupid
things. I lose my temper or—"

"Well, fortunately, you didn't lose her," his father
said from behind him in the doorway. Neither of
them had heard Huck, so she didn't know how long
he'd been standing there.

Her husband surreptitiously wiped at his tears but
didn't get up. Nor did he let go of the one hand he
held of hers too tightly.

"In fact, son, she looks like she feels much better," Huck said as he entered the hospital room. "But
you should have gotten those jars from the garage
when she asked you to. I'm sure you won't make that
mistake again."

Wade squeezed her hand even tighter. "No, I
won't," he said, his voice sounding strained. "I
swear."

"Then let's get this woman home. Can't let crime
run rampant because of peach jam," Huck said with
a laugh.

Wade got up slowly as if he had a terrible weight
on his shoulders. Abby watched him use the wheelchair arms to support himself as he lumbered to his
feet.

She'd blamed his job at the sheriff's office for
the change in her husband, but as she felt the ten-

sion between Wade and his father, she wondered
how much of the change in him was Huck's doing.
Her father-in-law often talked about making his son
a man. It was no secret that he thought Wade wasn't
"tough" enough.

The doctor came in then to talk to her about her
recovery. He still questioned whether she should be
going home. She could tell that he was worried about
her—and suspicious of her accident.

But Abby found herself paying more attention
to what was going on out in the hallway. Huck had
drawn Wade out into the hall. She couldn't hear
what they were saying, but just from her husband's
hunched shoulders, she knew that Huck was berating
him. Talk about the kettle calling the skillet black,
she thought.

"STOP YOUR DAMNED BLUBBERING," Huck said, taking
Wade's arm and halfway dragging him down the corridor. "You didn't do anything wrong, remember? So
quit apologizing."

"Easy for you to say," Wade said under his breath.

"You need to be more careful. If the doctor had
overheard you…" His father shook his head as if
Wade was more stupid than he'd even originally
thought. "On top of that, the nurse said that Ledger

McGraw stopped by to see your wife after you left," Huck said.

Wade swore and kicked at a chair in the hallway. It skittered across the floor, before Huck caught it and brought it to a stop with a look that told him to cool it. Wade wanted to put his fist through the wall. "He just won't stay away from my wife."

"So what are you going to do about it?" Huck asked, sounding as angry as Wade felt.

"I'm going to find the son of a bitch and kill him." He smacked the wall hard with his open palm. The pain helped a little.

"This is your problem—you go off half-cocked and just screw things up," his father said. "Listen to me. You want to get rid of him? I'll help you, but we won't be doing it when you're out of control. We'll plan it. As a matter of fact, I have a way we can be rid of Ledger McGraw and the rest of them, as well."

Wade stared at his father. "What are you saying?" He narrowed his eyes. "This is about the long-standing grudge you hold against Travers McGraw."

"What if it is? I don't just whine and cry. I take care of business."

He shook his head at his father. "I know you said you used to date Marianne before she married Travers, but—"

"But nothing." Huck wiped a hand over his face,

anger making his eyes look hard as obsidian. "She was *mine* and then he had to go and marry her, and look how that turned out."

"You might be crazier than she is," Wade muttered under his breath, only to have his father cuff him in the back of the head as they headed back to Abby's room.

ABBY LISTENED TO the rain on the roof for a moment before she realized that she was alone. She rolled over to find the bed empty. More and more Wade was having trouble sleeping at night.

He'd said little after bringing her home from the hospital. Once at the house, he'd insisted she go to bed. He'd brought her a bowl of heated canned soup. She'd smelled beer on his breath, but had said nothing.

"I'll let you get some rest," he'd said after taking her soup tray away.

Sometime during the night she'd felt him crawl into bed next to her. She'd smelled his beery breath and rolled over only to wake later to find his side of the bed empty.

Now she found him sitting outside on the covered porch. He teetered on the edge of the chair, elbows on his knees, head down as if struggling with the weight of the world on his shoulders.

Abby approached him slowly, half-afraid that she might startle him. His volatile mood swings had her walking on eggshells around him. The floorboards creaked under her feet.

Wade rose and swung around, making her flinch. "What are you doing?" he demanded gruffly.

"I woke up and you weren't in bed. Is everything all right?"

"I just needed a little fresh air. You don't have to be sneaking up on me."

Abby desperately wanted to reach out to him, to comfort him, to plead with him to tell her what was making him so miserably unhappy. She blamed herself. They'd been good together once. Hadn't they?

But clearly he was in no mood for the third degree. Also she'd learned to keep her distance when he was drinking. But she knew he was hurting. Because of her fall? Or because of something else?

It was raining harder now. She hugged herself, the damp seeping through her thin nightgown. There'd been a time when he would have noticed just how thin the fabric was, how it clung to her rounded breasts and hips. Back then he would have pulled her to him, his breath warm against her neck. That husky sound in his voice as he told her how much he wanted her, needed her. How he couldn't live without her.

Wade didn't give her another look as he sat down again, turning his back to her. "You should go to bed."

She felt tears burn her eyes. Wade kept pushing her away, then losing his temper because he thought some other man might want her.

"I saw Ledger McGraw looking at you when you came out of the grocery store," Wade would say. "I'm going to kill that son of a—"

"You can't kill every man who looks at me," she would say.

"You like it when he looks at you."

She would say nothing, hoping to avoid a fight, but Wade would never let it go.

"He wants you. He isn't going to give up until he tears us apart. Not that he would ever marry you. He had that chance already, remember? Remember how he lied to you, cheated on you—"

There was nothing she could say to calm him down. She knew because she'd tried. "Wade, don't be ridiculous."

"Right, I'm ridiculous. I'm no McGraw, am I?"

"I married *you*."

"Only because you couldn't have Ledger."

She would try to hug him and he would shove her away, balling his hands into fists. "You never got over him. That's what's wrong with our marriage. You're still yearning for him. I can see it in your eyes."

He would shove her or grab her, wrenching her arm. It would always end with him hurting her and then being sorry. He would berate himself, loathing that he was now like his father. He would promise never to do it again, beg her forgiveness. Plead with her not to leave him.

And each time, she would forgive him, blaming herself for setting him off. Then they would make love and it would be good between them for a while.

At least, that was the way it used to be. Lately, it took nothing to set Wade off. And there was no pleading for forgiveness or any making up afterward.

"It isn't like anyone else wanted to marry you," her mother told her when she'd seen Abby wince from one of Wade's beatings. Her mother loved to rub salt in the wounds. "It's plain to see that you aren't making him happy. You'd better do whatever it takes or he's going to dump you for a woman who will. Then where are you going to be? Divorced. Left like a bus at the Greyhound bus station. No man will want you then."

Abby had bit her lip and said nothing. She'd made her bed and now she had to lie in it. That was her mother's mantra.

"And stay clear of that McGraw," her mother had

warned. "Men always want you when you're with someone else. But the minute they get you, they lose interest. So don't be thinkin' the grass is greener with him. You already know you can't trust him. Look how he broke your heart. Just be glad Wade was willing to marry you since you weren't exactly white-wedding-dress material, now, were you?"

Now she stared at the back of her husband's head for a moment, then padded barefoot back to bed. If only she could remember how she'd gotten hurt. She had a feeling that would have answered all of her questions about what was happening with her husband.

"ABBY'S STARTING TO REMEMBER," Wade told his father the next day. He'd been relieved that he had to work. The last thing he wanted to do was sit around with her. He felt as if he was going to come unraveled at the seams as it was. She knew she hadn't fallen off a ladder. He saw it in her eyes and said as much to Huck.

"So what? It isn't like she's going to tell anyone," his father said. "If she was going to do that, she would have done it a long time ago."

"She's going to leave me."

Huck swore. "She would have done that a long time ago, too. She's fine. It's you I'm worried about."

"*Everyone* knows." As he'd wheeled Abby out to his patrol car parked at the emergency entrance, he'd seen the way the nurses were looking at him. Everyone knew now that he was his father's son—a bastard who mistreated his wife. He was thankful he and Abby hadn't had a kid. What if he took his anger inside him out on his *own* son?

"Snap out of it!" his father barked as they stood talking by their patrol cars. "You're in the clear."

Wade shook his head. "I'm afraid she's going to remember why we fought. If she remembers what she overheard you and me talking about…"

"I thought you said she didn't remember *anything*?"

He shrugged. "She says she doesn't, but the way she looks at me… She's going to start putting it together. I can see it in her eyes."

"Bull. If she remembered, she'd either go to the sheriff or she'd be in your face. What she needs to do is get back to work, keep her mind off…everything. In the meantime, you need to stay calm. You can't mess up again."

"I'll treat her real good," he said more to himself than his father. "I'll make up for everything."

"That alone will make her suspicious. Do what you normally do."

"Get drunk and stay out half the night?" Wade

asked his father in disbelief. "And you think that will help how?"

"It won't make you seem so desperate. Stop saying you're sorry. It was her damned fool self who climbed up that ladder to get those canning jars."

Wade stared at him. He'd always known that his father bought into his own lies, but this was over the top. "She's not *stupid*. She knows damned well she didn't fall from a ladder." He felt a sob deep in his chest begging to get out. He wasn't sure how much longer he could hold it together. "You don't live with her. You have no idea what it's like. She knows she can do better than me. She's always known. If she ever finds out that we lied to her about Ledger McGraw and that girl at college—"

Huck swore a blue streak. "Stop feeling sorry for yourself, you miserable little miscreant. It's our word against McGraw's. He swore nothing was going on, but if she didn't believe him then, she sure isn't going to now. She isn't going to find out unless you confess everything. She married *you*. Don't blow this. If she remembers what we were talking about when she overheard, then we'll deal with it. In the meantime, go get drunk, get laid, stop worrying."

ABBY COULDN'T SIT STILL. The doctor had told her to rest, but she felt too antsy. Not being able to remember nagged at her. She got up and turned on the television.

Standing, she flipped through the channels, but found nothing of interest and turned it off.

Out of the corner of her eye, she saw a book lying open on the floor next to her chair. As she bent to pick it up, she winced at the pain in her ribs. Dizzy, she had to grab hold of the chair arm for a moment.

She stared at the book, trying to remember. Had she been reading? It bugged Wade when she read instead of watched television with him. He took offense as if her reading made him feel dumb. It made no sense. No more sense than what had happened to her. Why would she have been reading if she was going to get canning jars down to make peach jam?

Marking her place, she put the book down and walked into the kitchen to open the refrigerator. Of course there were no peaches in there. Had she really thought there would be this time of year? Her ribs hurt worse as she breathed hard to fight back the nausea. She hadn't fallen off a ladder. Why did she keep trying to make Wade's story plausible?

She turned to look at her house, seeing her life in the worn furniture, in the sad-looking cheap artwork on the walls, in the creak of the old floorboards under her feet.

Her gaze went to the floor as she caught a whiff

of pine. Someone had cleaned the kitchen floor—but not with the cleaner she always used. Wade? Why would he clean unless...

Heart beating hard, she noticed that he'd missed a spot. She didn't need to lean any closer to know what it was. Dried blood. *Her* blood.

ABBY REALIZED SHE had nowhere to go. But she desperately needed to talk to someone. Even her mother.

She knew she shouldn't be driving, but her house wasn't that far from her mother's. Once behind the wheel she felt more in control. Seeing the blood, she'd quit lying to herself. She hadn't fallen off a ladder. Wade had hurt her. Again. Bad enough for her to end up in the hospital.

Only she had no idea why, which terrified her.

Too upset to just sit around waiting for Wade to get off his night shift, she'd finally decided she had to do something. If only she could remember what they'd fought about. A vague memory teased at her, just enough to make her even more anxious. It hadn't been one of their usual disagreements. It hadn't even been Wade drunk and belligerent. No, this time it had been serious.

As she turned down the road, she saw the beam of a flashlight moving from behind her mother's house toward the old root cellar. Abby frowned as her mother and the light disappeared from view.

Why would her mother be going down there this time of the night? She pulled up in front of the house and got out. As she neared the back of the house, she saw that her mother had strung an extension cord so she would have light down in the root cellar. It would be just like her mother to get it into her head to clean it out now, of all crazy possible times.

Abby had spent years trying to please her mother, but she felt she'd always fallen short. She almost changed her mind about trying to talk to her tonight. Her mother would be furious with her for not believing her husband—even though it was clear he was lying. Nan Lawrence was a hard woman to get close to. The closest they'd been was when her mother had pushed her to marry Wade after her breakup with Ledger McGraw. Not that it had taken a whole lot of pushing since she had been so heartbroken.

She'd just reached the back of the house and was about to start down the path to the root cellar when she heard a vehicle. A set of headlights flashed out as the car stopped in the stand of cottonwoods nearby. Someone had just parked out there.

Her first thought was Wade. He'd stopped by the house to check on her, found her gone and figured she'd run to her mother.

Hanging back in the deep shadow of the house, she watched a figure come out of the woods. It was too dark without the moon tonight to see who it was, but it was definitely a man, given his size. Wade? He stopped for a moment at the opening to the root cellar before lifting the door and disappearing inside, leaving the door ajar.

Although she couldn't make out his face, she caught the gleam of a badge on a uniform. Abby almost turned back. She wasn't even sure she wanted to see her mother now that she was here. She definitely didn't want to see her mother and Wade. They would gang up on her like they often did, confuse her, make her feel guilty for not being a better wife. Make her believe that all of it was her fault.

And yet she was tired of running away from the truth. Wade had almost killed her. There couldn't be another time. Not unless she had a death wish.

She moved toward the open door of the root cellar. Wade had left it open. A shaft of light rose up out of the earth as she walked toward it. Her head ached and she told herself now wasn't the time to have it out with her husband.

But her feet kept moving, like a woman headed for the gallows.

The moon was still hidden well behind the cloud

cover. She made her way across the yard until she reached the gaping hole of the root cellar.

The room belowground was larger than most root cellars. Having lived in Kansas as a child, her mother was terrified of tornadoes. No amount of talking had convinced her that tornadoes were rare, if not unheard of, in this part of Montana. She'd insisted that her husband build it large enough that if she had to spend much time down there, she wouldn't feel cramped. So he had. He'd have done anything for her. No wonder he'd died young after holding down at least two jobs all of his life.

Abby braced herself on the open door and took the first step, then another. The steps were solid. Also she could hear voices below her that would drown out any noise she made. They wouldn't hear her coming. She thought she might hear them arguing, but as she got closer, she realized there was only a low murmur rising up to meet her as if they were speaking in a conversational tone.

That alone should have warned her.

It wasn't until she reached the bottom step that she saw she'd been wrong about a lot of things. The man with her mother wasn't Wade. Nor was her mother down here cleaning.

Abby froze as she took in the sight. Black lights hung from makeshift frames along the earth ceiling.

Under them green plants grew as far back into the root cellar as she could see.

Her mother and her visitor had frozen when they'd seen her. Deputy Sheriff Huck Pierce had a plastic bag filled with what looked like dried plants in his hand. Her mother had a wad of cash. Both quickly hid what was in their hands.

"What are you doing here?" her mother demanded. "You never stop by and tonight you decide to pay me a visit?"

Realization was like a bright white noise that buzzed in her aching brain. She stood stock-still. This, she realized, was why her mother had pushed her to marry Wade. It had nothing to do with him being her best choice. No, it was all about his father and the drug business her mother had been secretly running in her root cellar.

"Abby," Huck said casually. "I thought you'd be home in bed."

"I'm sure you did," she said and looked to her mother.

A mix of emotions crossed Nan's face before ending with resignation. "So now you know," she said.

Yes, now she knew why her mother had berated her for not being a better wife to Wade. Even when Abby had told her how Wade hurt her, she hadn't said, "Leave the bastard." No, she'd told Abby that it was her fault. That she needed to treat him better. That she needed to put up with it. Otherwise, she would be a divorcée, and look how that had turned out for her mother after Abby's father had died and she'd quickly remarried twice more and was now divorced again.

"I'll let you handle this," Huck said as he moved to leave. He tipped his hat as he edged past Abby as if she was a rattlesnake that couldn't be trusted not to strike.

But it wasn't Huck who she wanted to sink her venom into. It was her mother. All she'd wanted was her mother's love, she realized now. But the woman was incapable of real love. Why hadn't she seen that before?

"Don't be giving me that look," her mother snapped as she put away the empty jar that had held the dried marijuana the deputy had just bought. "I have to make a living. That's all this is. You have no idea what it's like being a single woman at my age. Anyway, it should be legal in this state. Will be one day and then I'll be out of business. But until then…"

She thought of all the things she wanted to say to her mother and was surprised when the only words that came out were "I'm divorcing Wade."

"You don't want to do that."

"*You* don't want me to do that, you mean. Or is it Huck who wants me to stay with his son?"

"Huck and I agree that the two of you need to work some things out. You two married just keeps things…simple."

"Simple for you since you're apparently in business with his father."

Her mother took a step toward her. "I won't hear any more about this. What are you doin' here, anyway? You should be home waiting for your husband. No wonder he has to take a hand to you."

Abby heard herself laugh, an odd sound down in the root cellar. "It's not going to work, Mother. All I've ever wanted was you to like me if not love me. I tried to do what you asked of me, thinking that one day…" She shook her head. "Don't worry. I'm not going to turn in your little…operation or snitch on the deputy. Knowing Huck, he'd wiggle out of it and let you fry. But as for you and me?" She shook her head again and turned to leave.

"You're making a huge mistake. You leave Wade and things will only get worse for you. I'll tell you what. Quit your waitressing job and come into business with me. I'll cut you in and—"

"Save your breath," she said over her shoulder. "You and I are finished."

"I'm your *mother*. You listen to me," Nan yelled after her.

"I'm through listening to you." Abby topped the stairs and stumbled out. She took huge gulps of fresh air and fought tears. All this time she'd been trying to do the right thing according to her mother. It had all been to keep a drug dealer happy? Her mother had never cared what happened to her. It hadn't been about her marriage vows at all.

She staggered through the dark to her car, her ribs hurting as she took each ragged breath. She half expected Huck to be at the edge of the darkness, waiting to leap out at her. But apparently he'd left, believing that her mother could handle her. Look how well she'd done so far.

The moon peeked out from behind a cloud, startling her. Abby held her breath until she was behind the wheel of her car, the doors locked. She sat for a moment, gasping between sobs, the pain deeper than even her bruised ribs.

She started the car, desperately needing to leave here. Looking behind her, she saw her mother come out of the root cellar and stand, hands on her hips in the dim moonlight, scowling as she watched Abby drive away.

Chapter Five

"I didn't expect you to be back to work already," Ledger said, eyeing Abby a week later. "Are you feeling all right?"

"I'm fine," she said, handing him a menu and placing a glass of ice water in front of him. The familiarity of it after all this time had a nice resonance. She realized that if he ever quit coming in, she would miss him terribly.

That thought made her feel guilty. She knew what Wade would make of it.

Since the night she went to her mother's, Wade had been an adoring husband. Abby was sure his father must have said something to him about what she'd seen in the root cellar. Was that why he was being so attentive? Because he was afraid she would tell?

But tell what? She hadn't been able to remember anything from her lost twenty-four hours. She'd wondered if it hadn't had something to do with Wade's father's illegal business with her mother. Was that what she and Wade had argued about?

She didn't think so. All her instincts told her it was more serious than that. It nagged at her. She feared it was something worse, but couldn't imagine what that would be.

Seeing Ledger made her forget for a moment about that part of her life. He had always brightened her days. She'd often regretted jumping into marriage with Wade, but had been determined to stick it out no matter what. She'd taken her marriage vows seriously— even without her mother's nagging.

"What would you like this morning?" she asked as Ledger picked up the menu. He had to have it memorized as often as he came in and the menu hadn't changed in fifty years except for the prices.

"Abby," he said, lowering his voice.

She fought the impulse to lean in closer. Close enough she could smell his distinct male scent, something that was branded on her memory. The soft sweetness of it was a painful reminder of when they'd been together. Ledger had been her first, something that Wade had never let her forget.

"I spoke to the nurse on your floor at the hospital. She told me that your injuries weren't consistent with a fall off a ladder."

"Ledger." The word came out a plea. He wasn't telling her anything she didn't already know. He couldn't keep doing this. It was killing her.

"I thought you should know. Wade lied to you."

Tears burned her eyes. She'd known Wade was lying to her the moment she'd seen his face. It wasn't the first time nor did she suspect it would be the last. But he was trying, something he hadn't done since becoming a deputy sheriff.

"He's going to kill you one of these days and then I'm going to prison for the rest of my life because I am going to tear him limb from limb." He said it so matter-of-factly that his words were like an arrow through her heart.

"Ledger. No."

"Why, Abby? Why have you stayed with him?" The pain in Ledger's voice made tears blur her eyes. She hadn't just been putting *herself* through this.

She shook her head. All her reasons for staying no longer mattered. She took a step back, then another, bumping into a table before she got turned and rushed back to the kitchen.

"Get control of yourself," her elderly boss snapped as she rushed into the kitchen in tears.

"I can't do this anymore," Abby cried.

Ella took a step toward her. "If you're quitting, you aren't quitting in the middle of a shift."

"I'm not quitting." She lowered herself to a stool by the back door, her face in her hands. "I can't keep going back and forth, even in my mind."

Ella stepped to her and placed an arm around her shoulders. "Honey, this has been coming for a long time. You can't be that surprised."

"I'm a *married* woman."

Ella snorted. "And Wade is a married man. You think that means much to him? Now wipe your face." She handed her a paper towel. "Honey, it's time to fish or cut bait. You're going to have to make a decision, and from where I'm sitting, it's pretty damned clear. You going to let Wade keep knocking you around? Or are you going to put a stop to it?"

She looked up, surprised, although she knew she shouldn't be. Of course her boss knew. "I've told him—"

"*Telling* him don't mean squat. Anything short of shooting him won't do any good if you don't leave him. I've held my tongue, but I can't anymore. Stop being a damned fool."

"But—"

"No buts. And stop listening to your mother. She doesn't have the sense God gave a goose. I'm telling you straight. Dump that man and get on with your life before you don't have a life. Now get back to work."

Abby went into the restroom and wiped her face. She'd cried enough over her situation. She looked as she came out to see that Ledger had left.

"I told him to get on out of here and to quit crowding you," Ella said. "You need to cut him loose if you don't have the sense to end your marriage. Now do what women have always done—buck up and get back to work."

VANCE COULDN'T BELIEVE IT. He looked around the bedroom thinking he had to be dreaming. He'd downplayed how poor his adoptive family had been or how hard he'd had to work or how much debt he had from college.

As he walked to the window to look out, he felt a stab of jealousy for Cull, Ledger and Boone. They'd grown up here. They'd had all this and more.

But now you're one of them.

"Not yet." There was the DNA test. He'd managed to put it off as long as he could, knowing it was just a matter of time before he'd be forced to take it.

In the middle of dinner tonight Cull McGraw and his girlfriend had shown up. Both had looked at him like he was a bug under a microscope as if searching for his fatal flaw—just as they had the first night he'd met them. The girlfriend, Nikki St. James, the true-crime writer, had wanted to see the stuffed toy horse that night. He had watched her inspect it and seen that the horse had definitely been the ticket in.

But it would all come down to the DNA test.

"When is the DNA test scheduled?" Cull had asked his father tonight.

Travers had seemed taken aback by his son's abruptness.

"No reason to put it off any longer, right?" Ledger had interjected.

Vance had met Travers's gaze. "They're right. No reason not to schedule it," he'd said with more confidence than he felt. One more major hurdle and then he was home free, so to speak.

But he remembered that first night well. "So what have you been doing since college?" Nikki had asked.

"You can interview him for the book some other time," Travers had said with an embarrassed laugh.

"Sorry, questioning goes with the occupation," she'd said, but he had known he'd have to answer a lot more questions before this was over.

That was why he'd answered it that first night. "I've been working on some ranches in southern Montana. I'm apparently good with horses." That had pleased Travers—just as he knew it would. Vance had smiled to himself as he'd finished his meal.

Now over a week later and alone in his room, he

tried to relax and enjoy how far he'd come. This was definitely an upgrade from how he'd been living, but, he reminded himself, it was temporary.

"How are you settling in?" asked a voice from the doorway.

He swung around to find the attorney smiling at him. "This place is beautiful."

Waters agreed as he stepped into the room and walked to the window to look out on the swimming pool, pool house and horse barns. Past them, the Mc-Graw ranch stretched to the Little Rockies. "Dinner went well again tonight, don't you think?"

"I guess."

The attorney shot him a look. "Is there a problem?"

"No, but I think it's time I took the DNA test. Until I do…"

Waters nodded. "I don't see any rush, but it's up to you. Travers has accepted you. You seem to fit this place and this family."

He wasn't so sure about that. He might have won Travers over, but he wasn't so sure about the others.

"Now it is only a matter of tying up the loose ends," Waters said.

He wondered if the attorney was referring to the DNA test or the five-hundred-thousand-dollar reward. "I was wondering… The reward money? The friend who pointed out that I might be Oakley... I want him to have it."

The attorney studied him for a moment. "Minus my ten percent, you mean. I'm sure that can be arranged. Do you want me to speak to Travers?"

"No, not until after the DNA test." He swallowed back the bile that rose in his throat. "Once there is no question that I'm Oakley..."

LEDGER CORNERED HIS brother Cull.

"What do you want me to say?" Cull demanded after listening to what his brother told him.

"He lied about Abby falling off a ladder," Ledger repeated with more force.

"*Wade Pierce lied? Hell, stop the presses.* What should we do? I know—let's go over to his house and beat the crap out of him. Is that what you want me to say?"

"That would be a good start. Not that I need your help."

"Yep, you should go alone, that way I'll be able to get you out of jail on bail after you've gotten the hell kicked out of you by both Wade and his worthless father, who is also a deputy. Good plan."

"What am I supposed to do?" Ledger demanded.

"Do I have to remind you that Abby isn't your wife, not your responsibility, not even your business?"

"I'm just supposed to let him keep hurting her?"

Cull sighed. "She chose him. I know that's hard for you to accept but—"

"You don't know her. She sticks with whatever she promises to do. She promised to love him until death they do part."

"Then that's probably what's going to happen."

"I'll kill him."

"Oh, damn," Cull said and dropped his head into his hands for a moment. "Okay, what do you want me to do?"

Ledger looked at a loss for words. "We have to save her."

His brother nodded. "Okay, I reckon we could kidnap her."

"Kidnap who?" Boone had come into the room but stopped at his words and looked at him as if he'd lost his mind.

"Abby," Cull said. "We could wait outside the restaurant about the time she got off work and just grab her and—"

"And go to prison for kidnapping?" Boone demanded.

"Wait, this isn't such a bad idea," Ledger said. "Once we get her away from him, she will come to her senses and—" He stopped, seeing their disbelieving looks, and realized Cull had been kidding.

"Haven't you been trying to convince her to leave him?" Cull asked. "Has it done any good?"

"It's…complicated."

"Isn't it, though? I hate to tell you this, little brother," Cull said. "But as hard as it is, you need to step off."

Ledger flopped down in a chair. "I can't do that."

"What choice do you have?" Boone asked. "She doesn't want you."

"That's blunt enough, thanks, Boone," Cull said sarcastically. "Where are you going?" he asked as Ledger got to his feet and headed for the door.

"I'm going to find Wade," he said as he approached the door.

"He's going to end up in jail," he heard Boone say behind him. "Or worse if Huck and Wade tag team him. You ought to stop him."

"I suppose we could hog-tie him in the barn, but eventually we would have to let him go and then what?" Cull said.

Ledger let the door slam behind him as he headed for his pickup.

"WHERE HAVE YOU BEEN?" Abby asked when Wade finally showed up at home later that night.

He jumped, startled to find her waiting in the dark corner of the porch. "You scared the devil out of me."

Somehow she doubted that.

"I asked where you've been."

"You'd better change your tone and right now," he said, but it wasn't with the same meanness in his voice. She really *had* scared him. The last thing he'd expected was to see her sitting in the dark waiting on him.

He reached in and turned on the porch light, blinked and then studied her as if trying to gauge what was going on.

"I'm still waiting," she said calmly.

"I was working," he said, starting to get belligerent. She could smell the beer on his breath from where she was sitting. But that wasn't the only scent she picked up on him. The cheap perfume turned her stomach.

She also noticed that he seemed to be swaying a little as if fairly drunk. Normally she wouldn't confront him. But tonight it was as if something had snapped in her. He'd been so good for weeks, but she'd known in her heart it wouldn't last.

"Don't bother to lie," she said, getting to her feet. "I know where you've been and what you've been doing." She started past him.

He grabbed her arm, spinning her around to face him. This was when she would normally hurriedly apologize, look at the floor, take whatever belittling he threw at her and then try to get away as quickly as possible.

Tonight she looked him in the eye with a fire she hadn't known she possessed. He seemed startled, his grip on her loosening a little.

Her gaze went to where his fingers clutched her arm. "Get your hands off me."

Amazingly, he let go. "You're getting some kind of mouth on you," he blustered. "You keep that up and I'll—"

"No, you won't," Abby said. She kept her voice calm but with an edge to it he'd never heard before because she'd never dared talk to him like this. "If you ever touch me again, you and I are done." She pushed past him, half expecting him to grab her from behind and backhand her.

But he didn't touch her. He let her go into the bedroom where she closed the door, the sound of the lock deafening in the house at this late hour.

Her heart was pounding like a war drum. She quickly moved away from the door, afraid he would charge it using his body like a battering ram and knock it down. The lock was fairly flimsy. It wouldn't take much.

But beyond the door she heard the shuffle of his heavy boots. He knocked over a lamp and cussed as it hit the floor. She heard him say, "I should bust down that door and teach that bitch what's what."

But with relief, she knew he wasn't going to do anything but pass out. She moved to the bed as she heard him collapse on the couch. Would he wake up in the middle of the night having sobered up just enough to be furious that she'd locked him out of his bedroom?

She climbed into bed, feeling the cold aluminum of the baseball bat she'd purchased in town. It lay next to her. She'd bought it on impulse today after work because as good as Wade had been, she'd known in her heart it wouldn't last.

Abby took hold of the bat. If he busted down the door and came in all raging fists and angry threats, he would get another surprise.

For a long time, she lay propped against the pillows, clutching the bat and waiting. Ella was right. She had to take control of her life. This was a start.

If she could save her marriage, she had to try. Ella was right about that. She was also right about Ledger. She needed to cut him loose.

Chapter Six

Last night Ledger had driven around Whitehorse, looking for Wade's pickup. The deputy hadn't been at work. He also hadn't been at any of the local bars.

While he'd thought about driving out to Abby's house, he had enough sense not to. The more he drove through the sleepy little Western town, the more he realized something had to change. He'd been carrying this torch for Abby since high school. If he'd married her when he'd had the chance, none of this would be happening.

But they'd been too young and he'd promised his father that he'd finish college before they married. Unfortunately, Abby hadn't been able to wait. He'd heard that she was pregnant with Wade's baby, but that hadn't been true. Instead, he suspected the rushed marriage had been Abby's mother's doing. That woman just wanted to get her daughter married off—didn't matter to whom, apparently.

He'd finally driven toward home, telling himself he had to stop going by the café on the mornings Abby worked. He upset her too much. He had to back off. His brothers were right, as hard as that was to admit.

Feeling as if his heart was breaking all over again, he drove home. As he got out of his pickup, he saw that his brother Cull was sitting on the porch as if he'd been waiting for him.

"You don't have to get me out of jail," he said as he climbed the porch steps.

"Glad to hear it. Not that I was waiting up for you," Cull lied.

Ledger smiled at him as he took a step next to him. "I drove around looking for Wade for a while."

"Must not have found him."

"Nope, but I did do some thinking. You're right. Abby knows how I feel. It's in her court now."

Cull reached over and clasped his shoulder to give it a squeeze. "I know how hard this must be for you. But you've done all you can at this point."

He nodded. "I love her."

"I know." Cull was quiet for a moment. "So you think this Vance Elliot is our brother?"

Ledger shrugged. "He looks like us."

"He does that. Says he's good with horses." Cull

chuckled. "I was thinking we'd put him on that new stallion."

Ledger actually smiled at that. "I'd pay money to see it."

Cull got to his feet. "It's late. Guess we'll know for sure when the DNA test results come back. I would imagine Dad will talk the lab into putting a rush on them. Or maybe not. I think he's enjoying the idea of Oakley being home. You going to be okay?"

"Don't have a lot of choice."

ABBY WOKE THE next morning, only her and the baseball bat in the bed. No Wade. He hadn't awakened in the night. Or if he had, he'd thought better about breaking down their bedroom door.

She realized that she felt better. Her ribs were still sore. She still had a dull ache in her head, but even it was better.

Rising, she dressed, and moving to the door, she slowly unlocked it. She had no idea what to expect. The wear and tear of living in a relationship where she had to walk on eggshells had taken a toll on her. She felt jumpy, unsure, afraid as she slowly opened the bedroom door, the doorknob in one hand, the baseball bat in the other.

The couch was empty. She stood listening before taking another step. Was he waiting for her in the hallway off the bedroom, planning to jump her the moment she came out?

With the bat in both hands, she started down the hallway. She took a few steps and stopped to listen. The house creaked and groaned, but there was no sound of Wade.

She could see the indentation in the couch where Wade must have slept at least part of the night. One of the couch pillows was on the floor.

Cautiously she moved down the hallway toward the kitchen. The floor creaked under her step. She froze and listened again.

Just a few more feet and she would be able to see into the kitchen. He would have had time to think about what she'd said to him last night.

She prayed that he would know she meant it this time and that if he didn't change she would leave him. But she knew that her ultimatum might just as easily set him off and make things worse between them.

If what Ledger had told her was true about people at the hospital knowing she hadn't fallen off a ladder? Word would spread fast and everyone in the county would know the truth about her and Wade. Shame burned her cheeks. They'd know her terrible secret. All her lies had been for nothing. Because this time

Wade had hit her hard enough that he'd had to take her to the hospital.

That story about her climbing the ladder in the garage for jars to make peach jam had been just that—a ridiculous story that he'd cooked up.

She shuddered as she realized that Wade hadn't come up with that on his own. His father's fingerprints were all over it. Wade would have panicked when he couldn't wake her up. He would have called Huck to ask him what to do.

Abby felt sick because all of it sounded so much more believable than the jam jar story. Yet she had wanted to believe it. Worse, she'd wanted Ledger to believe it.

What was wrong with her? She'd let her husband hurt her, telling herself that he was under a lot of pressure because he'd lost his job or because he wanted to make good at the sheriff's department or because he'd had a rough day at work. Like she'd never had one of those.

When he'd lost his temper and hit her, she'd told herself it was her fault. She'd promised to try harder to please him—just as her mother had said.

A wave of disgust washed over her as she moved to the doorway to the kitchen and stopped.

Wade was sitting at the table, elbows on the tabletop, his head resting in his hands. A floorboard must have creaked, because he suddenly lifted his head and turned it in her direction.

His eyes were red and shiny. Hungover? Or crying? She couldn't tell. Either, though, could change in a heartbeat and turn violent.

Those eyes focused on her, shifting from her face to the bat in her hands. His expression went from sorrowful to surprised, then deeply hurt. She realized he'd been crying. It was what he always did after he hurt her. She'd never doubted that he was sorry or that he didn't want to hurt her again. Until the next time.

"Abby?" His voice sounded lost.

She shifted the bat to one hand and let it rest against her leg.

"You don't need that," he said, still sounding shocked that she would either think that she needed a bat to protect herself or that she would consider hitting him with it.

She felt the irony of that soul-deep.

Yesterday she'd been determined to save her marriage. But looking at him sitting there, she knew that she no longer wanted to. The last few months had been so much worse than any she could have imagined. Him putting her in the hospital because of his temper... It was the last straw.

"I want you to pack your things and move out,"

she said, surprised how calm she sounded. Her heart was pounding in her chest.

"Abby, you can't mean—"

"I do, Wade. I can't live like this." He had started to get up, but her words stopped him. He settled back in the chair and put his head in his hands again.

"Don't do this, Abby. I'll change. I swear I will. In fact, things are going to get better."

The familiar words had no effect on her. She stared at her husband and wondered how long it had been over. She'd left him once. That night, running for her life, she'd made the mistake of going to her mother's.

"Don't you ever darken my door again. Your place is with your husband."

"You don't understand. He's going to kill me." She had pleaded with her mother.

"What did you do?"

She'd stared at her mother in disbelief. "I didn't do anything."

Her mother sneered. "You did somethin' to make him mad."

"He came home drunk, smelling of some other woman—"

"Grow up, Abby. He's a man. He has to let off a little steam. Be glad he took some of it out on that other woman before he got home. You want to be a good wife? Don't make him mad. Now get out of here. He finds out you came here…"

She'd left, walking home in the dark and realizing she had no other place to go than back to Wade.

Now she felt a sadness deep in the pit of her stomach. She hadn't been strong enough to leave Wade then, but she was now. "It's over, Wade."

"You can't throw me out of my own house," he said belligerently. But he didn't make a move toward her.

She felt the weight of the bat. "If you don't leave, I'll call the sheriff. I don't think you want that."

He fisted his hands at his waist, glaring at her. Then knocking over the chair, he jumped up and stormed out. She listened to the sound of his pickup engine dying off in the distance before she went to the door, locked it and pushed the fallen chair under the knob.

But all her instincts told her he wouldn't be back. At least not until tonight.

WATERS SHOWED UP the next morning to see if Vance needed a ride to the lab for his DNA test.

"This really isn't necessary," Travers said when he opened the door to see his attorney standing there.

"I'm representing Vance through this," Waters

said, surprising his old boss. "He asked me to on his behalf. I hope you don't mind."

"I guess I can understand how he might feel alone in this, though if this test comes back like I think it will, he'll now have family to take care of things. I hope, after all these years, that you won't be involved in any litigation with my son."

"I was the one who brought him to you," Waters reminded him. "I promised to look after his interests even though I've spent years looking after yours. But I'm sure once we confirm he's your son that he will have everything he needs."

Travers nodded.

"Since I am only on a retainer with you, I thought you'd appreciate me taking care of things on his behalf."

"You know I do." The horse rancher turned as Vance came down the stairs.

Just moments before, Waters was feeling good. Travers did appreciate what he was doing. He thought they might actually be able to patch things up. He was about to breathe a sigh of relief when he saw Vance's expression.

Worry wormed through him. The kid looked petrified. Maybe he hated needles. Waters could only hope that was all that was going on with Vance. Surely he wouldn't be so stupid as to think he could pass a DNA test if he knew he wasn't Oakley McGraw.

Then again, maybe Vance thought the toy stuffed horse would be enough.

He tried to relax. The kid had the horse. Unless he'd picked it up at a garage sale, he was Oakley McGraw, right?

"I thought you and I would ride together to the lab," the attorney said to him. He promised to see Travers and his sons at the lab and quickly steered the would-be Oakley outside.

Once the two of them were in the car, he buckled up and looked over at the kid. "If there is some reason you think you might not pass this DNA test, then you need to tell me now."

ABBY WONDERED WHAT had made her think she could stay in this house. Everywhere she looked there were too many bad memories. Her first thought this morning was simply getting away from Wade. She didn't think her body could take another run-in.

But once she realized she didn't want to stay here, she knew she had to find a place of her own. Something small. Something she could afford by herself.

They'd been paying on this house for the past couple of years. If there was any equity in it, Wade could have it. She just wanted out.

That decided, she couldn't wait to pack up and leave. It wouldn't take much packing. She hadn't accumulated hardly anything she cared about over these few years of marriage.

When she looked around, she thought she could pack all of her possessions into the two suitcases out in the garage. She walked through the kitchen, opened the door from the house to the garage and froze.

A memory tugged at her the moment she saw the ladder lying on the garage floor. Was it possible she *had* fallen—just as Wade had said? She shook her head. No, the blood was in the kitchen. But there was something about the garage and the ladder.

Standing there, she tried hard to remember. Closing her eyes, she felt another nudge. Wade and his father. She frowned. They'd both been in the garage. She'd come to the door and heard them talking.

A shudder moved through her. Why had they been talking in the garage? Because they hadn't wanted her to hear. But she *had* heard. Had she let them know it?

Apparently not at once since she'd found her dried blood on the kitchen floor. Had she confronted Wade about what she'd heard and the argument had gone from the garage to the kitchen?

She squeezed her eyes closed tighter. They'd argued, but she'd already suspected that. But not in the garage. No, it had been in the kitchen. The two of them alone. But what had it been about?

Something important. Had Wade found out that she'd gone back on the pill and had been keeping it from him? She shook her head and tried to concentrate on what she'd seen and heard in the garage.

She could almost see Wade and Huck with their heads together, talking in grave tones in the garage. Almost hear… She opened her eyes with a groan, the memory just out of her grasp. But whatever it was, it was serious.

WATERS HAD FOUND a local lab to do the DNA test so they didn't have to travel out of town.

"Won't you need to get DNA from Mother?" Ledger asked. Once they'd seen that Jim Waters would be taking Vance to the lab, he and his brothers had insisted on driving their father.

"At this point, all they need is mine," Travers said after lecturing them about babying him. "It should be conclusive enough. If needed, we can get your mother's."

As they walked in, Ledger wondered how long it would be before the news was all over town. He'd already heard the rumor going around that one of the twins had been found. Waters's doing? Or Vance's?

Vance had spent his first night in a motel in town. If Waters had checked him in, that could have been enough to get tongues wagging.

At the lab, his father walked up to the reception desk and was told that he could come on back. As he disappeared down a short hallway, Ledger looked around. The building was small. His brothers had taken seats in the waiting area, but he was too antsy, so he'd moved where he could see down the corridor.

There were a series of small rooms off the hall. His father had gone into one of those with the lab tech. He wondered where Vance was. At the sound of a familiar voice, he saw Deputy Sheriff Huck Pierce step out of one of the rooms with one of the lab techs, this one a redhead. She was laughing at something the deputy had said.

Ledger turned away, but not before he'd seen the lab tech move to open the door of one of the rooms. He got a glimpse of Vance sitting nervously on a gurney, waiting to have the test done. He didn't look like a man who believed he was Oakley McGraw.

"Good thing Dad is smart enough to demand a lab test," Ledger said when he joined his brothers. "I just saw Vance. He looks scared to death. What if he's lying?"

"Then we'll know soon enough," Boone said. "DNA doesn't lie."

"He had the toy stuffed horse." Cull shook his head. "What I want to know is what happens if he *is* Oakley."

Chapter Seven

Ledger let a few days go by before he stopped in the Whitehorse Café. He halted at the door to scan the room as he always did. Today, he would tell Abby why he hadn't been back. He would apologize for making things worse for her. He would step off.

But as always, there was that moment of expectation, that sense of hope, then concern when he looked around for her. If he didn't see Abby, there was always a painful disappointment that ruined his appetite. But he was too polite to turn around and leave on those days when she'd traded shifts. He would have a little something to eat even though the other waitress could tell there was only one reason he'd come in and it wasn't for the food.

"Abby took the day off," her friend Tammy said as she swung by on her way to a table with two plates full of biscuits and gravy. She didn't give him a chance to comment.

Abby never took a day off unless something was wrong. He waited until Tammy came back to ask, "Is she all right?"

Tammy slowed to a stop even though he could tell that she was really busy this morning. He saw her hesitate. He knew she didn't like telling something that Abby might not want him to know.

"It's okay," he said, not wanting to put her on the spot. "She needs loyal friends."

"She's looking for an apartment," Tammy said and gave him an encouraging smile.

"An apartment?"

"A studio," she said pointedly and then took off as she had another order come up.

A studio apartment. Did that mean what he hoped it did? That she'd finally left Wade? He tried to keep from getting too excited about the prospect, not knowing what it meant. There was always the chance she would change her mind. Or worse, that Wade would stop her.

He couldn't possibly eat a thing. He left and walked to his pickup, his step lighter than it had been in three years.

He'd just climbed into the ranch pickup when his cell rang. He thought for a moment that it would be Abby calling with the good news. He reminded himself that he wasn't part of the equation. He hadn't been since she married Wade. Just because she was getting an apartment—

Ledger quickly dug out his phone, still hoping. "Hello?" he said without checking to see who was calling.

"You need to get home," his brother Cull said without preamble. "Dad just got the DNA test results. He wants us all there."

"That quick?" Ledger asked in disbelief.

"They did just a preliminary one that should tell us if Vance Elliot has any of our blood running through his veins."

"I'm on my way." He disconnected and sat staring out over the steering wheel. It was the moment of truth.

He started the truck and drove as quickly as he could toward the ranch, his thoughts straying radically from what was waiting for him at home to what Abby was doing right now.

He wanted to call her, but he resisted. He'd promised himself he would give her space. Ledger chuckled to himself, thinking about the times he'd wanted to pull some crazy romantic stunt like he'd seen in the movies. He'd ride into the café on his horse, scoop Abby up and ride off into the sunset with her. He'd save her from herself, from Wade, from her horrible mother.

Ahead the ranch came into view, the Little Rockies in the distance. He slowed the pickup to turn down the road past the bright white wooden fence that lined both sides of the road. A half dozen horses had taken off in the wind, their manes flying back as they ran.

The sight always made him smile. He loved this ranch, loved raising horses. He'd always thought that he would bring Abby here after he saved her.

Waters's car was parked in front of the house along with an older-model pickup he didn't recognize. Vance Elliot's?

Both trepidation and excitement filled him. For twenty-five years his father had searched for the twins. Was it possible the DNA test would prove that one of them had finally made his way home?

ABBY FELT STRONGER every day both physically and emotionally. She'd made a point of ignoring the pleading messages her mother left on her phone as well as the angry, threatening ones.

To her surprise, Wade had stayed away, as well. Each night she had expected him to get a snoot full of beer and come banging on her door. When she woke each morning to realize he hadn't, she felt like a woman in the eye of the hurricane. She didn't kid herself that it would be this easy to get her freedom from him.

Now she braced herself. The last couple of days had been nice not having to confront him. Unfortunately, she had to talk to him. She found Wade as he was getting off his shift. From the look in his eyes, his father had already told him everything, including that Abby now knew about the marijuana business.

"We should talk about all this at home," Wade said once he was close enough to whisper.

"I don't have that much to say and I don't want to be alone in the house with you." She saw the sharp ache of pain in Wade's eyes. The other times, she'd weakened. "I moved out of the house today. You can keep it or sell it, whatever you want. I don't want anything from you."

"You don't mean that. You're just angry and upset. Once you calm down—"

"No, Wade. I do mean it and I'm not going to change my mind. It's over between us."

A muscle jumped in his jaw. He got that familiar look in his eyes. If they hadn't been standing on the street in front of the sheriff's office, he would have lost his temper and they both knew what happened then.

"I saw a lawyer today and filed separation papers. There is a waiting period, but once it's over, if you sign the divorce papers, you won't have to pay for a lawyer of your own. Up to you, but dragging this out will only cost us both money."

He stared at her as if he couldn't believe the words out of her mouth. "You just hold up a minute. You didn't say nothin' about no divorce."

"I told you I was done."

"That ain't the same as a divorce," he said, taking off his Stetson to rake his fingers through his hair. "I just thought you needed some time to cool off."

"No, Wade. I can't be married to you anymore. Please don't put up a fight. It's over and I'm not going to change my mind."

He put his hat back on, looking like he was going to cry. "I'll change. You have to give me another chance."

"I've given you too many chances," she said, looking away from him.

His voice broke and, when she looked at him, fury was back in his gaze. "It's McGraw. Ledger McGraw."

"Believe what you want because you will anyway, but this is only about you and me." She started to walk back toward her car, hoping he wouldn't come after her.

But, of course, he did. "Abby, I know I've messed up…"

"Please stop," she said, continuing to walk. "I

don't want to rehash this. You know exactly why I'm divorcing you. I won't tell anyone about how you physically abused me unless you fight the divorce."

She heard the breath come out of him in a whoosh. Clearly, he hadn't thought about that. Not that people didn't know already. Ledger had always known. But it was clear that Wade liked to think it was still their secret.

"It's my word against yours," he said, grabbing her arm and spinning her around to face him.

She jerked her arm free. "People saw the bruises on me, Wade. They'll testify in court. The doctor at the hospital is already suspicious after my…accident."

He looked furious but also scared. If it became public knowledge, he could lose his job. He grabbed her arm again.

"You're hurting me," she said, keeping her voice down. He released her arm and stepped back as if he didn't trust himself. "Just let me go. It's for the best. And, Wade? Don't let your father make you do something stupid."

"What does that mean?"

"My mother and your father have their own selfish reasons for wanting us together. I wouldn't take their advice." With that, she opened her car door and climbed in to roll down the window. "My lawyer will have the paperwork to you soon. Just sign it and let's part amicably, okay?"

She didn't give him a chance to answer as she turned the key in the ignition and drove away. He was still standing there looking after her when she pulled onto the street. They would never be *amicable*. She would be lucky if he gave her the divorce, let alone left her alone. No, she thought, fighting tears. She'd be lucky to get out of this alive.

LEDGER WATCHED THE celebration feeling strangely outside it. After twenty-five years, one of the twins was back. It was more than surreal. He glanced at his father. Travers looked so happy it made his heart ache with joy. But he was the only one, Ledger thought as he surveyed the family. They all looked as stunned as he felt.

He saw Nikki watching Vance. Or did they now start calling him Oakley? Nikki was sharp; that was what made her such an excellent true-crime writer. She saw things that other people missed. And she knew people. Look how much she'd uncovered in a very short time recently.

She was frowning as she studied Vance. Ledger wasn't sure he could call him Oakley, even if the twenty-five-year-old would answer to it after all this time.

His father was suggesting another bottle of champagne as he put an arm around his long-lost son. Vance just looked uncomfortable in his new role.

Ledger moved closer to Nikki in time to hear her whisper to Cull, "Something's wrong."

His brother sighed. "He has the toy," Cull said quietly. "He has our blue eyes. He looks like us. But more to the point, he passed the preliminary DNA test with flying colors. So what are you saying?"

Nikki shook her head and looked to Ledger. "You feel it, don't you?"

He nodded. "It just feels…"

"Wrong," Boone said, joining them at the edge of the party.

Just then their father called them over so he could fill their champagne glasses.

"Whatever it is all of you think you know, keep it to yourself," Cull warned them. "Look at Dad. He's happy. So I'm happy. It will take some time, but let's make the best of this."

MEMORY IS A *funny thing*, Abby thought. One minute her mind nagged at her to remember what had happened that night in the garage and later in the kitchen. The next, she would get a flash. Just enough to make her stop what she was doing to try to hang on to it before it disappeared again.

She'd realized that she was missing one of her fa-

vorite earrings. Knowing that Wade should be working and away from the house, she'd driven out to look
for the earring.

It was while down on her hands feeling around
under the bed for the earring, when her fingers closed
on it, that she had her strongest flash yet. She froze
as the memory came to her like the trailer of a movie.
She saw Wade and his father in the garage, their
heads together in serious conversation. But this time,
she heard what they were talking about.

At the sound of a vehicle pulling up in the yard,
Abby jerked up, banging her head on the bed frame
as she drew back, the earring biting into her fingers.
Her head swam for a moment from the pain, from
the memory, from the sound of a car door closing
and heavy footfalls on the porch steps.

She rose and looked out the bedroom door toward
the front of the house. At the sound of a key in the
lock, she knew it had to be Wade. He would have
seen her car parked out front.

Abby looked around as if for a way to escape.
But the bedroom window was painted shut and she'd
never be able to get down the hallway to the back
door without being seen. If Wade saw her trying to
get away from him, it would only make it worse.

Indecision froze her to the spot. She felt sick to her
stomach from what she'd remembered. She wished

she'd never remembered. Just as she wished she had forgotten about the earring. She should never have come back here.

But she realized that knowing what she now did, she would have to go to the sheriff. She had no choice. Wade wasn't a good husband. He had a miserable temper and he often struck out when he was hurt or mad or drunk, which was often. But she'd never thought he was a bad man. She'd often felt sorry for him, knowing how he was brought up by his father.

But after what she'd heard Wade and his father discussing in the garage… Once she went to the sheriff, she would never be safe. If Wade didn't get her, his father would. She would be just as good as dead. Her only other option would be to stop Wade before he and his father went any further—as if anything she could say would convince her husband to go against his father.

She'd forgotten all about her earring until she heard it hit the floor. She hadn't even realized it was still in her hand until she'd dropped it. Bending down, she felt around for it in the dim light of the bedroom. She'd just recovered it when she heard a floorboard creak behind her.

"Abby?"

She hadn't heard him come down the hallway. Now he was standing in the bedroom doorway.

He saw the look on her face and swore. "You remembered."

Now she really was trapped.

Chapter Eight

Abby backed away from her husband. She'd never seen such fear and fury in his eyes before.

"You are going to keep your mouth shut. Is that understood?" he demanded as he advanced on her, matching each of her steps with one of his own until he backed her into a corner.

"Wade, I'm begging you not to do this," she said, trying to keep the tremor out of her voice and failing.

"Begging?" He laughed. "I like the sound of that."

"I'm serious. I've gone along with a lot since we married, but this—"

"This is our ticket out of this hellhole. Come on, don't pretend that you wouldn't like a nice big house like the McGraws'." He snickered. "Just the mention of that name and your eyes sparkle, but it's not the house you crave, is it?"

"Please, don't start on that."

"Don't even want to hear Ledger McGraw's name on my lips, do you?"

She bumped hard against the wall. He had her trapped and he knew it. She'd put up with so much from him in the time they'd been married. At first he'd been so sweet, so understanding. He'd put her on a pedestal, but then he'd been fired at his feedlot job. His father had gotten him on as a sheriff's deputy and Wade had changed. He'd become more like the father he'd told her he despised.

He was close enough now that she could see the fire burning in his dark eyes. He desperately wanted to hit her.

Why had she tried to reason with him the night before he'd put her in the hospital? Why hadn't she gone straight to the sheriff when she'd found out what he and his father were up to?

Too late now. If only she could reach the gentle man who often cried in her arms after hurting her.

"Ledger McGraw," he repeated, his mouth twisting in an angry sneer. "I think my saying his name hurts you more than if I was to knock you into next week."

"Wade, this isn't about Ledger. This thing you're planning is cruel and illegal."

"Illegal?" He guffawed. "Honey, did you forget who you're married to? I'm a frigging deputy sheriff. There ain't nothing illegal when I'm carrying my badge and gun."

She feared he believed that. It would explain the change in him since becoming a deputy. She'd been a fool to provoke him by trying to change his mind. Even if she backed down, she had his ire up. He was going to hurt her.

And then what? Suddenly she wasn't sure how far he'd go to keep her from telling what she'd overheard him and his father planning.

"I NEED YOU to come right over," Wade said into the phone, his voice breaking.

His father swore. *"What did you do?"*

He glanced over the body lying on the floor. "It wasn't my fault but I might have hit her too hard."

His father swore again. "Don't do anything, you dumbass. Just stay there. I'll be right over," he said before slamming down the phone.

Wade hung up and rubbed a hand over his face. Then pulled it away, shuddering as he saw it was covered in blood. He quickly wiped it on his pants.

"Stupid, stupid, stupid," he said, hitting his forehead with his palm. Why did he let it go so far? Why didn't he just walk away before it got so bad? Maybe he could have talked some sense into her. Why did he have to take it out on her?

"Because I'm my father's son," he said in disgust.

Walking over to Abby, he squatted down beside her. She didn't look that bad. His old man had taught him not to hit a woman in the face. Didn't want the neighbors talking or, worse, someone down at the sheriff's department being forced to call him on the carpet because everyone in town had seen his wife's black eye.

But he must have hit her in the face this time because her nose was bleeding and after her concussion...

His back door banged open. Angry footfalls marched down the hallway. He turned as his father came storming into the room.

"She still alive?" Huck asked.

"I don't know."

"You didn't check?" He let out an angry snort and, shoving Wade out of the way, squatted down to check her pulse. "You lucked out, you worthless little prick. She's still breathing. How long has she been out?"

Wade looked around as if the answer was in the room. "I don't know."

His father rose and glared at him. "What are you doing beating on her again?"

"You mean like you used to hit me and Mom?"

"Watch your mouth, smart boy," he said, stepping to him. Huck grabbed him by the front of his shirt and slammed him against the wall. "Why pick a fight with her today, of all days? Do I have to remind you that we have too much at stake for you to be calling attention to yourself with the authorities again because of some petty argument with your old lady? What were you thinking?"

"It wasn't petty," he gasped out. His father was choking him with the balled-up shirt at his throat. "She *knows*." He wiped a hand over his face, smelled her blood on him still and rubbed his palm against his jeans.

Huck let go of him and took a step back. "How?"

He shook his head. "I don't know. She must have just remembered. She'll tell."

Huck swore and turned to look at the woman on the floor. "We don't have any choice, then. We can't take her back to the hospital. I know someone who's an EMT. We can take her to him. He'll cover for you, and if she's smart, she'll keep her mouth shut and go along with it."

Wade bit at his cheek. He hated to tell his father but he didn't think Abby would be going along with anything anymore.

"It may take more than that," he said quietly.

Huck turned to look at him. "What are you saying?"

"I don't think she's going to keep this to herself. Not this time."

His father took a step toward him. Wade raised

his arms to protect his head and waited for the force of Huck's punch to knock him to his knees.

Abby moaned.

Wade peeked from under his arms, surprised his father hadn't struck him.

"We'd better decide what to do with her," Huck said. "But first, you have any whiskey? I could use a drink."

ABBY DIDN'T KNOW how long she'd been lying on the floor bleeding. She groaned and tried to sit up. Her ribs protested violently and she had to lean back against the side of the bed. The room began to spin and she thought she might throw up. She closed her eyes, fighting the nausea. She could hear Wade and his father in the kitchen. From the clink of ice in the glasses, it sounded as if they were having a drink.

How was that possible with her lying in here on the floor, fading in and out of consciousness? Or had, this time, Wade thought he'd killed her?

They had lowered their voices, but she could make out most of what they were saying since this house was so poorly insulated. Her head ached. She had to concentrate hard to understand the words.

"...get rid of her body...have to do it tonight... can't just dump it anywhere."

Fear spiked through her. They couldn't be talking about getting rid of her. Getting rid of her for good. But even as she thought it, she knew it was true. Wade had gone too far this time. He thought he'd killed her.

She realized that he couldn't take her back to the hospital or questions would be asked. He might lose his job. He loved being a sheriff's deputy. He'd never give that up just because this time he'd hit his wife too hard.

Abby caught hold of the edge of the bed and pulled herself up. She realized she'd left a bloody handprint on the spread. For a moment, she stared at it, thinking the spread would have to be soaked to get that out.

A noise in the other room brought her back to the pain in her body, the ache in her head. She felt dizzy standing and wasn't sure how much longer she could stay upright.

Get out before it's too late, a voice screamed in her head.

She worked her way to the door and looked out. She could still hear Wade and his father in the kitchen. They were talking in very low tones now. She only heard the occasional clink of a glass or an ice cube.

They would be coming back for her soon.

She looked toward the back door. It seemed too far away to reach given how dizzy she felt, but she started for it, moving at a snail's pace as she used the wall for support.

She felt dazed, not even sure she was awake as she reached the door and tried the lock. Unlocked. It felt slick in her hand as she turned the knob and the door swung open.

A cool breeze hit her in the face, and from some survival instinct older than time, Abby knew she had to run for the trees now. If the men in the kitchen felt this breeze, they'd know she'd opened the back door. They would know that she was trying to get away.

She ran, the first step jarring her ribs and making her hurt all over. She ran bent over, her arms wrapped around her middle as if she could hold herself together. She didn't look back. She didn't dare. She had to believe she could reach the trees. She didn't think past that.

Abby stumbled on a tree root, lost her balance and went down hard. The fall knocked the air out of her and hurt her already aching ribs. She rolled over on her back and lay there, gasping like a fish out of water.

Over her head, stars glittered, making her think she was blacking out again. Her vision cleared as she caught her breath. She lay there listening, expecting Wade and Huck to find her and that her painful run for safety had only been a waste of time and effort.

Hearing nothing, she was suddenly aware of the weight of her cell phone in her pocket. She pulled it out, but for a moment, she couldn't think who to call.

Not her mother. Not her friends. She couldn't drag them into this. Wade had already warned her what he would do to them. As she held the phone, she felt a sob rise in her chest.

There was only one person she could call. She got up and stumbled deeper into the woods. She thought for a moment that she wouldn't be able to remember his number. But it was right there when she touched the keypad. She prayed he hadn't changed his cell number as she waited for it to ring.

The first ring filled her ear, making a sob escape. She held her breath as it rang a second time. "Please answer. Please."

She had no one else to turn to. She couldn't call the sheriff where Wade and Huck were both deputies. They would talk their way out of it even if she were believed.

It rang again. He wasn't going to answer. She gripped the phone tighter, feeling all hope slipping away.

She was just about to give up when Ledger answered on the fourth ring.

She began to cry so hard with such relief that she couldn't speak.

"Abby?"

She managed to get out two words. "Help me."

He didn't hesitate. "Just tell me where you are."

"SHE'S GONE!" WADE CRIED as he rushed back into the kitchen, where his father was finishing off the last drop of whiskey in the bottle. Fortifying himself for what had to be done.

"What do you mean, she's gone?" Huck demanded, slamming down his glass.

"She's not lying in there where we left her. There's blood on the spread and on the wall outside the room…"

"Come on, she can't have gotten far in her condition."

Wade returned to the bedroom, checked the bathroom and even looked under the bed.

"This way, you fool," his father snapped.

As he stepped out of the bedroom, he saw the handprints along the hallway. They led straight to the back door, which was standing open.

"What are we going to do?" Wade cried. He'd had just enough whiskey that he felt warm inside, but his head felt fuzzy. Everything about this felt surreal.

"She can't get far on foot," Huck said after checking to make sure she hadn't taken one of the cars.

"We would have heard her start up the engine, if she had."

Wade headed for the stand of cottonwoods along the creek behind the house. It was a straight shot from the back door and seemed the obvious place to try to hide.

He hadn't gone far, though, when he found her shoe. It lay on its side next to the creek. He whistled for his father to join him as he looked deeper into the dark shadows of the trees.

I'm going to find her out here dead. That thought immobilized him until he heard his father's heavy footfalls behind him.

"There's her shoe," Wade said, pointing at it.

"Pick it up. She must be close around here." Huck started to step past him.

"I don't think so," Wade said, holding him back with his free arm. He shone his flashlight on the tracks past the shoe. "They look fresh," he said of the tracks.

Huck bent down. "Someone picked her up and carried her." He glanced past the creek and the cottonwoods to the dirt road on the other side. "She have her phone with her?"

Wade swore under his breath. "You can damn well bet who she called. Ledger McGraw."

Huck rose right in front of his son. "You screwed

this up royally. I could…" He reared back, but Wade blocked the punch.

"I'm not that boy you used to knock around," he said through clenched teeth. "You can call me a fool, you can say whatever you like, but if you lay another hand on me, I'm coming after you."

Huck scowled at him. "You think you can take me? You punk."

"Don't know but I'm going to try."

Huck laughed. "Tonight isn't the time to find out. If she goes to the sheriff—"

"She won't. She's gone to Ledger McGraw. If anyone comes looking for me, it will be him and I'll be ready."

Chapter Nine

Ledger could think of only one thing. Take Abby to the hospital and then find Wade. He'd never been violent, but seeing what Wade had done to Abby had him to the point where he thought he could take the man's life. Wade had to be stopped and if it meant ending him...

"Where are you taking me?" Abby asked from the passenger seat of the pickup. He could tell that each word hurt her to speak. He would have brought the Suburban so she could lie down in the back but he hadn't known how badly she was hurt.

"To the hospital," he said.

"No!" She tried to sit up straight but cried out in pain and held her rib cage. "That's the first place he'll look for me."

"Abby, you need medical attention."

"Please."

He quickly relented. He couldn't let Wade near this woman, which meant no hospital. At least for now.

"I'll take you to the ranch and call our family doctor. But, Abby, if he says you have to go to the hospital—"

"Then I'll go." She lay back and closed her eyes. "I didn't want you involved."

"I've always been involved because I've always loved you."

She said nothing. He could tell that she was in a lot of pain. It had him boiling inside. If he could have found Wade right now...

He slowed to turn into the ranch and called Dr. Johns. His service answered. Ledger quickly told the woman what had happened. "We need him to come out to the McGraw ranch." She put the call through. Doc asked a few questions about her condition.

Ledger answered best he could.

"I think you should take her to the hospital. I can meet you there."

"She doesn't want to go to the hospital because her husband can find her there. I'm taking her to the ranch."

"Then I'll meet you there."

Ledger pulled up in front of the house. He saw that she was looking at it, tears in her eyes.

"This is not the way I ever wanted to come back here," she said.

"I know. But right now the only thing that matters is that you're here and safe."

"Promise me you won't go after Wade." When he didn't answer right away, she cried, "Ledger, please. I can't bear the thought of losing you."

"I promise," he said, although they were the hardest words he'd ever had to say.

ABBY REMEMBERED LITTLE of the ride to the ranch or Ledger and his brothers helping her to a bed upstairs. The doctor had apparently told Ledger not to let her sleep because he stayed with her, asking her about everything but what had happened until the doctor got there.

It wasn't until the next morning, when the doctor told her she could sleep now, that Ledger asked, "Do you want me to call your mother?"

"No!" She'd looked so stricken that he hadn't pushed it as the doctor left.

"Is there anyone else I can call?"

She shook her head, tears filling her eyes. "He's already told me what he'll do to my friends if I involve them."

Ledger gritted his teeth, his anger a rolling boil inside him. What the man had done to Abby... But when he spoke, he sounded calm. "Okay, you just rest. Everything is going to be all right." As he started to turn from the bed, she grabbed his hand.

"You can't do anything to Wade. You can't let him know where I am. If you do anything... You promised."

He nodded as if he'd already figured that out for himself, but she could tell he wasn't happy about it. "Don't worry. He won't know where you are."

"Oh, he'll know," she said. "But he wouldn't dare come out here." Wade didn't operate that way. He would wait until she left here. He would wait until he could catch her alone.

And when that happened, she had no doubt that he would kill her. She'd done the unforgivable in his eyes. She'd gone to Ledger McGraw.

MCCALL TOOK ONE look at Abby and wanted to take a two-by-four to Wade Pierce. Locking him behind bars wasn't enough.

"How are you feeling?" the sheriff asked as she took the chair next to the woman's bed.

The changes going on at the house had surprised her. She'd heard that there had been quite a lot of renovation since Patricia was arrested and never coming back.

But McCall knew that wasn't all there was to it.

With one kidnapper identified and now dead, the money recovered and news that the twins had been adopted out to eager families through a member of the Whitehorse Sewing Circle, Travers seemed to have a new lease on life.

For twenty-five years, he'd kept the children's rooms and the entire wing of the house just as they were the night of the kidnapping. As if freed of some of the past pain, he was opening up the rooms and redecorating them.

The room where Abby was staying looked as if everything in it was brand-new. The walls had a fresh coat of a pale yellow. The curtains billowing in the faint breeze were light and airy. It was as if the room had been decorated just for her.

"I'm feeling better."

McCall could tell that it was going to be hard for her to open up and talk about what had been going on. Abby had tried to keep the secret, no doubt out of shame. McCall had run into this before. Often an abused woman never wanted anyone to know, blaming herself as her husband also did.

"Do you remember what happened?"

Abby shook her head and seemed to realize that McCall would think she was covering for Wade. "The doctor said having another concussion so close after the first one has caused even more memory loss."

"The first one? The fall from the ladder?"

Abby looked away. "That's what Wade told me."

"I spoke with your doctor. You need to know that he reported the incident as physical abuse. This time I think you realize that something has to change, right?"

Tears filled the young woman's eyes as she nodded. "I had left Wade, moved into an apartment in town and filed for a separation, the first step in the divorce proceedings. I remember going out to the house to get something." She frowned. "Wade must have come home early." She shook her head. "I'd told him earlier in the day that he would be getting divorce papers and to please sign them."

McCall nodded. "Abby, do you remember calling 9-1-1 and telling the operator it was urgent that you speak to me?"

She felt her eyes widen. Had she called 9-1-1 as a threat to Wade if he came near her? "I don't remember calling."

"The operator said you told her that you'd discovered something horrible that your husband and his father were doing."

She shook her head as she thought of her mother's marijuana operation. Surely she wouldn't have called the sheriff on her own mother. It was something Wade and his father were up to? She had a glimmer of a memory but it only made her head hurt worse. "I'm sorry. I don't remember calling and I can't imagine what I was calling about."

McCall nodded. "I think it's time you filed a complaint against Wade. Will you do that?" When Abby hesitated, the sheriff added, "And I wish you'd also take out a restraining order against him. True, it isn't worth the paper it's printed on if Wade ignores it and comes after you, but the order will tell him you mean business—especially if you call 9-1-1 the moment he breaks it." Both of them knew he would break it.

Abby closed her eyes for a moment. "I'll do it. The complaint and the restraining order." She opened her eyes and met McCall's worried gaze. "He'll lose his job, won't he?"

"Not right away, but once he breaks the restraining order, yes. When Wade first got on at the department he seemed to have so much potential. He was really excited about the job. I'd had hopes for him. This is his wake-up call. I hope he takes it. In the meantime, I just want to keep you alive."

Abby chewed at her lip. "Wade's just so angry right now about me leaving him."

"It's even more dangerous now. The operator heard Wade in the background before you disconnected. She heard him say something like, 'You'd get me sent to prison? Your own husband?' Whatever you tried to tell me about Wade and his father, it sounds serious. If they thought you might remember..."

THE SHERIFF DIDN'T need to tell Abby how much trouble she was in. Wade had almost killed her. She vaguely remembered hearing him and his father in the kitchen, their heads together. They'd been talking about what to do with her body.

She shivered at the thought, suddenly restless. The room where Ledger had brought her was beautiful, but she couldn't stay here forever. Then what?

Even with the restraining order McCall had her sign, she knew Wade would come after her. He'd told her that if she ever left him, he'd kill her and then himself. She'd never doubted that. But he'd also told her that if she ever went to Ledger, he'd kill him, as well.

Her heart pounded at the thought of what she'd done by calling him. But last night there'd been no one else. She knew Ledger would come and get her. She knew he would take care of her. If she had hoped to survive, she had to get away from Wade and his father last night. Otherwise...

Climbing out of the bed, she felt a little dizzy for a moment but needed to move. She felt anxious and afraid. Ledger had promised he wouldn't go after

Wade. She had seen how hard it was for him to do that. She trusted that he would keep his promise.

But Wade coming after Ledger… Not that Wade would come out to the ranch. He wasn't that stupid. No, he'd wait until he could get Ledger alone.

She felt a memory pull at her. Something about the garage. It slipped past, refusing to let her grasp it long enough to make any sense of it. Wade and his father had been up to something that would send them both to prison if caught?

Abby felt sick to her stomach. What had the two gotten involved in? Something that apparently they would kill to keep quiet, she thought, remembering them whispering in the kitchen. The hair stood up on the back of her neck. If she hadn't gotten out of the house last night when she did, she'd be dead and buried out in the middle of the prairie.

McCALL TOOK NO pleasure in calling Wade Pierce into her office. When she'd hired him, she'd hoped he would make a better deputy than his father. He had seemed to have that potential. But maybe his upbringing was harder to overcome than she'd hoped.

He tapped at the door and stuck his head in when she said, "Come in, Wade. Please have a seat." Not surprisingly, he looked nervous. He had to know what this was about.

"I wanted to give you a heads-up," she said once he was seated. "Your wife has filed a domestic abuse complaint against you—" She held up her hand, seeing that he was about to argue the point. "As well as a restraining order."

The man looked dumbstruck. He really hadn't expected she would do that. Then he looked furious.

"I want to make something perfectly clear. Right now I'm suspending you for two weeks without pay so you can think about your life and any changes you might want to make. However," she said quickly as again he was half out of his seat, mouth open and ready to argue. "However, if you break the restraining order or if there is another call from your wife, you will be dismissed."

"But it's a lie." He wasn't very convincing and she could see that he knew it.

"I don't take these kinds of charges at face value. I spoke with her doctor at the hospital. After that, I advised your wife to take these steps not just for her sake but for yours."

Wade shifted his gaze to look down at his boots. "So two weeks."

"This is serious, Wade. You can end up behind bars. If there is no trouble between now and then, I'm willing to give you another chance here. Anyone else I would have let go. Tell me that my faith in you isn't misplaced."

He looked up and swallowed, his Adam's apple bobbing up and down for a moment. "There won't be any trouble."

"Good. I'm glad to hear that. Wade, get some help." She slid a pamphlet across the desk to him.

"Anger management?" He let out a nervous laugh.

She saw his father in him then and knew she was probably wasting her breath. "Often this problem is generational. But it can be stopped."

"Generational," he repeated and frowned. He looked again at his boots. "Right."

"That's all."

He got up slowly, his hat in his hand. She could see that he was fighting all of this, going from embarrassment to anger and back. She feared anger would win.

"You know this will get all over town," he said quietly.

"Wade, everyone already knows what's been going on. Now's your chance to show them what kind of man you are."

He nodded slowly. "Two weeks." And walked out, closing the door a little too hard behind him.

Chapter Ten

"I thought you said she'd never go to the sheriff," Huck Pierce demanded when Wade found him at his house and told him the news.

"She didn't. Apparently the sheriff went to her. It's that doctor at the hospital. The sheriff said he suspected physical abuse and reported it."

"So much for patient privacy," his father snapped.

"Isn't he required by law to report it? Maybe that's what happened."

"Or maybe your wife's boyfriend is behind all of this."

Wade ground his teeth. "As far as I know, she's still out there."

"Well, she can't stay there forever. I asked around. I found out where the apartment is that she rented."

"The sheriff was real clear. I can't go near her or I'll be fired."

"Well, there's no restraining order against me,

but you're right. Now isn't the time to be worrying about this. We have bigger fish to fry." He winked at Wade. "Our plan went off without a hitch. Now it's just a matter of waiting for the money to roll in. Once you don't need this job anymore, you can get your wife back—if that's what you want."

"I'd rather die than see her with McGraw."

His father smiled. "That's what I thought. Believe me, she won't be for long."

LEDGER COULDN'T BELIEVE how different the house felt with Patricia and Kitten gone. But it was even better now, he thought, that Abby was free of Wade.

The biggest change in the mood at the McGraw ranch, though, was one of the twins being found. Vance had settled in upstairs in the wing where he'd once lived as a baby.

It had surprised Ledger when his father had announced that the wing would be remodeled. No longer would it be a shrine to the kidnapped children. Instead, it would be made into quarters for Vance— and eventually Jesse Rose, once she was found.

"You do realize that Jesse Rose might have a life she doesn't want to leave," Boone had pointed out. "She'll be twenty-five years old. She might not want to move back into the house where she was kidnapped."

It seemed odd to the three older brothers that Vance would move in. But he apparently had little going on in his own life and this had been his home.

"I'm aware of that," his father had said with a laugh. "But I want them to feel at home here on the ranch. I want them to have a place. Oakley might not end up staying, but he will at least know that he has a room here."

"Oakley?" Cull had asked. "Is he going to change his name?"

"We're discussing it. Of course, it would be an adjustment for him," Travers had said.

Ledger thought Vance would be up for whatever his father wanted. He seemed to have adjusted quite well to living on the ranch. Earlier, he'd seen him at breakfast putting away any and everything set before him. Later he was down at the pool swimming and napping in the sun.

"He said he had a way with horses," Boone pointed out. "When is he going to start working?"

Their father sent his son a disapproving look. "He's just getting used to being Oakley McGraw."

"Oh, I think he's gotten used to it quite well," Boone said, getting to his feet. "If you want me, I'll be in the horse barn. Working."

Cull rose, as well. "He has a point, Dad. Maybe

you should discuss with Vance…Oakley what is expected of him." With that, he left.

Travers looked to Ledger. "Aren't you going to give me your two cents' worth, as well?"

"I think they pretty much covered it. I'm going into town to get a few things from Abby's apartment for her. You don't mind her staying on for a while, do you?"

"Of course not. Just be careful. Putting yourself in the middle of these kinds of things is very dangerous, especially with Wade Pierce."

Ledger nodded. "I'm not going to do anything stupid."

"But I don't think you can depend on Wade Pierce not to."

He smiled at his father. "I'll be careful."

As he started to leave, his father said, "I want to just enjoy having my son back for a while. But I don't want the rest of you resenting him. Am I wrong?"

Ledger turned at the door. "It's an adjustment for all of us. You just got him back. I don't think you need rush it."

His father smiled. "I could say the same about you and Abby."

He laughed. "Yes, you could, but you'd be wasting your breath. I'm going to marry that woman just as soon as she's free."

WATERS LISTENED TO Patricia McGraw's latest threat and realized he would have to go to the jail and have this out in person. It wasn't something he was looking forward to. He hadn't seen her since her arrest. He probably could have gone the rest of his life without seeing her. But she wasn't having any of that and somehow she'd hired herself a fairly good lawyer.

As Patricia was brought in, he picked up the phone. From the look in her eye, he was glad to have the thick, scarred Plexiglas between them. She sat down, glaring at him for a moment, before she picked up her own phone.

"You bastard," she said into the receiver.

"Nice to see you, too, Patricia. I'm a busy man, so if you have something to say, please do it."

She sneered. "I heard you're buttering up Travers so you don't lose your job. Good luck with that." He smiled and saw steam come out of her ears. "He's just stupid enough to keep you on. And what's this about Oakley being found?" she demanded.

He shrugged. "Seems that way."

She heard the suspicion in his answer and he could have kicked himself. "You think he's a fraud?"

"No. He looks like his mother, has the McGraws' blue eyes and dark hair."

YOUR PARTICIPATION IS REQUESTED!

Dear Reader,

Since you are a lover of our books – we would like to get to know you!

Inside you will find a short Reader's Survey. Sharing your answers with us will help our editorial staff understand who you are and what activities you enjoy.

To thank you for your participation, we would like to send you 2 books and 2 gifts – **ABSOLUTELY FREE!**

Enjoy your gifts with our appreciation,

Pam Powers

SEE INSIDE FOR READER'S SURVEY

For Your Reading Pleasure...

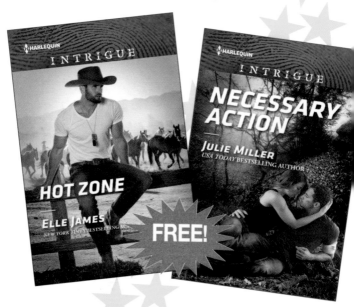

We'll send you 2 books and 2 gifts
ABSOLUTELY FREE
just for completing our Reader's Survey!

YOUR READER'S SURVEY
"THANK YOU" FREE GIFTS INCLUDE:
▶ **2 FREE books**
▶ **2 lovely surprise gifts**

▶ **PLEASE FILL IN THE CIRCLES COMPLETELY TO RESPOND**

1) What type of fiction books do you enjoy reading? (Check all that apply)
○ Suspense/Thrillers   ○ Action/Adventure   ○ Modern-day Romances
○ Historical Romance   ○ Humor   ○ Paranormal Romance

2) What attracted you most to the last fiction book you purchased on impulse?
○ The Title   ○ The Cover   ○ The Author   ○ The Story

3) What is usually the greatest influencer when you <u>plan</u> to buy a book?
○ Advertising   ○ Referral   ○ Book Review

4) How often do you access the internet?
○ Daily   ○ Weekly   ○ Monthly   ○ Rarely or never

5) How many NEW paperback fiction novels have you purchased in the past 3 months?
○ 0 - 2   ○ 3 - 6   ○ 7 or more

YES! I have completed the Reader's Survey. Please send me
2 FREE books and 2 FREE gifts (gifts are worth about $10 retail).
I understand that I am under no obligation to purchase any books,
as explained on the back of this card.

❏ **I prefer the regular-print edition**
182/382 HDL GLY5

❏ **I prefer the larger-print edition**
199/399 HDL GLY5

FIRST NAME	LAST NAME

ADDRESS

APT.#	CITY

STATE/PROV.   ZIP/POSTAL CODE

READER SERVICE—Here's how it works:

Accepting your 2 free Harlequin Intrigue® books and 2 free gifts (gifts valued at approximately $10.00 retail) places you under no obligation to buy anything. You may keep the books and gifts and return the shipping statement marked "cancel." If you do not cancel, about a month later we'll send you 6 additional books and bill you just $4.99 each for the regular-print edition or $5.74 each for the larger-print edition in the U.S. or $5.74 each for the regular-print edition or $6.49 each for the larger-print edition in Canada. That is a savings of at least 12% off the cover price. It's quite a bargain! Shipping and handling is just 50¢ per book in the U.S. and 75¢ per book in Canada.* You may cancel at any time, but if you choose to continue, every month we'll send you 6 more books, which you may either purchase at the discount price plus shipping and handling or return to us and cancel your subscription. *Terms and prices subject to change without notice. Prices do not include applicable taxes. Sales tax applicable in N.Y. Canadian residents will be charged applicable taxes. Offer not valid in Quebec. Books received may not be as shown. All orders subject to approval. Credit or debit balances in a customer's account(s) may be offset by any other outstanding balance owed by or to the customer. Please allow 4 to 6 weeks for delivery. Offer available while quantities last.

▼ If offer card is missing write to: Reader Service, P.O. Box 1341, Buffalo, NY 14240-8531 or visit www.ReaderService.com ▼

BUSINESS REPLY MAIL

FIRST-CLASS MAIL   PERMIT NO. 717   BUFFALO, NY

POSTAGE WILL BE PAID BY ADDRESSEE

READER SERVICE
PO BOX 1341
BUFFALO NY 14240-8571

NO POSTAGE
NECESSARY
IF MAILED
IN THE
UNITED STATES

Patricia made a face. She never liked the mention of Travers's first wife. "But?"

"No buts. He passed the preliminary DNA test. Travers is convinced and Vance seems to have settled into your house just fine."

She let out a growl. "Vance?"

"Oakley. I think he'll be changing his name soon. So we have a happy ending."

"Maybe you do. Listen to me. I'm not going down alone, you hear me? I promised my lawyer that you will be helping finance my defense."

"You what?"

"You're in this up to your neck. Unless you pony up some money…" She smiled, no doubt seeing how uncomfortable he was with what she was saying.

"You can't drag me into this."

"Jim, darlin', I have dates and times. I have phone messages. I have phone calls. I have enough that my lawyer assures me you will go down as an accessory—if not the person who actually bought the poison and administered it. You were there almost every meal. Did you really think you could frame me for this?"

"I didn't frame you. This is all you."

"I don't think so, Jimmy." She hung up the phone

and stood, smirking down at him as if she thought she had him by his private parts.

What killed him was that he feared she did.

ABBY COULDN'T HELP being nervous. Ledger hadn't returned from town. He'd taken one of the ranch hands with him to drive his pickup back after getting what she needed from her apartment and picking up her car at the sheriff's department.

"I want someone with you in case—"

He'd stopped her. "Wade is in a lot of trouble. He's not going to do anything that would get him thrown in jail."

She wasn't so sure about that. The sheriff had called to let her know that Wade had been warned—and that the restraining order would be served within the hour. On top of that, Wade had been suspended for two weeks without pay.

Abby couldn't even imagine how furious he was. It would only get worse when the restraining order was served—and he told his father.

"He's going to want to kill me—and you," she'd told Ledger before he left. "I shouldn't have involved you in this. I'm so sorry."

"Hey," he'd said, lifting her chin with his warm fingers until their gazes met. "I've been involved since the day I fell in love with you all those years ago. I couldn't let go. I know I should have but once I saw how he was treating you…"

"That's why you need to be careful. Give him time to cool down."

She had smiled at the man she'd loved for as far back as she could remember. So many times she'd regretted her hasty marriage to Wade. She knew now that Ledger would never have cheated on her. But back then she had her mother and Wade telling her different. She'd been afraid that the reason Ledger had put off marriage was because he didn't love her enough.

When she'd seen the photos of Ledger with some other woman at college…

She knew now that Ledger and the woman had just been friends. Her mother had wanted her with Wade for her own selfish reasons.

"I've made such a mess of things," she'd said, hating that she sounded near tears. She'd cried way too long over Wade and the mistake she'd made.

Ledger had cupped her cheek. "It's nothing that can't be rectified. I just want you to be sure of what you want to do now. I don't want to talk you into anything. Whatever you do, it has to be your decision. So maybe you should take this time to—"

"I've already filed papers to begin divorcing Wade. He knows it's over. I'd kicked him out of the house and I had packed up my things and moved them into the apartment in town. I guess I'd gone back to the house for something. I didn't expect him to be there…"

"That's all behind you, then." He'd leaned down and given her a gentle kiss. She'd wanted to pull him to her and kiss him the way she'd often dreamed— and felt guilty about. But it was too soon.

She'd jumped into a bad marriage. If she and Ledger had a future… Well, they could take it slow.

"As I was saying, I really think you should stay here for a while longer. I could go to your apartment and get you whatever you needed."

"My car is out at the house. I don't want you going out there."

"Why don't you call the sheriff and have some-one bring your car into town for you," Ledger had suggested.

She'd agreed and made the call. McCall had said that was smart not to send Ledger out to get it, or worse, go herself.

"I'll have the keys here at the sheriff's office."

"Ledger will be picking it up," she'd told McCall.

"This afternoon would be good since Huck isn't working."

Yes, she didn't want Ledger running into Wade's father, either.

"Thank you for doing this," she'd said to Ledger as she'd hung up.

"Don't you realize by now that I would do anything for you?"

She'd smiled. "I do."

But he wasn't back yet and all she could think was that he'd run into Wade. Maybe even Wade and his father.

She got up, too nervous to stay in the room any longer.

OAKLEY MCGRAW. "OAKLEY MCGRAW." Down the hallway from Abby's room, Vance stood in front of the mirror and tried out the name. His new name. When Travers had asked him if he had considered changing his name to his birth name legally, he hadn't known what to say. Maybe because he never thought it would get this far.

"Oakley McGraw." He was Oakley McGraw. He wanted to pinch himself. Two weeks ago he was Vance Elliot, ranch hand. All of his belongings were in his beat-up, rusted-out pickup. He barely had a job let alone a nickel to his name.

Now he was Oakley McGraw, son of Travers McGraw, heir to all of this. Along with three brothers, he reminded himself. Three brothers who he could tell didn't like him. As if he cared. Their father adored him.

That was why he was going to tell him he wanted to have his name changed to Oakley McGraw legally. Then there would be no question, would there. He would be the missing son. Travers was even thinking about throwing a party to introduce him to his friends. His friends were powerful people in this town, in this state.

Vance couldn't believe his luck. He looked out his window at the swimming pool shimmering in the sun. Maybe he would go sit down there in the shade after he helped himself to a beer from the refrigerator in the kitchen. That he had the run of this place was unbelievable. He thought he could live like this without any trouble.

As he started down the hallway, a door opened at the other end and a young woman stepped out. The cook had mentioned that there was a friend of Ledger's staying in the house. Apparently the friend had her meals brought to her, though, since he hadn't seen her before. He'd thought she must be a "special" friend.

He let out a silent whistle when he saw her. Even from a distance, she was real pretty. She hadn't seen him yet, so it gave him time to study her. As she drew closer, her gaze on the floor at her feet as if distracted by her thoughts, he saw that she had a black eye and other bruises.

Also she was walking as if in some kind of pain. Clearly, something had happened to her. A car accident? A mugging? An assault? This explained why she'd been eating in her room—and Ledger eating with her.

He hadn't realized that he'd stopped just short of the stairs to stare at her. She must have sensed him, because her gaze came up quickly and he got his first good look at her. With a shock he realized that he recognized her. Wade Pierce's wife.

Worse, she recognized him. Her blue eyes widened in alarm. She stumbled a little, but caught herself. "I'm sorry. You startled me."

"Sorry." He waited, heart in his throat, expecting her to say more.

But she only stared at him, recognition in her eyes and yet… He realized that she was trying to place where she knew him from.

"Please, you go first," he said, motioning to the stairs.

She shook her head. "I wasn't going down. I was just stretching my legs." She took a step backward and another, before she turned and went back down the hall the way she'd come.

He watched her, knowing it was just a matter of

time before she remembered where she'd seen him. All he could think was that when she did, she was going to take all of this away from him.

Chapter Eleven

Wade was surprised to see Abby's car gone when he drove out to the house. Had she come out to get it? Or had that bastard Ledger McGraw retrieved it for her?

He pulled up in front of the house, threw the car into Park and sat just staring at where her car had been. He should go out to the McGraw ranch and drag Abby out by her hair. Frustration had him shaking all over. He couldn't do that any more than he could get her back. His dad was right. He'd have to bide his time if he wanted any satisfaction. Look what the woman had done to him. He wouldn't be able to hold his head up in this town ever again.

He turned off the engine and started to get out when he remembered the restraining order. He couldn't come any closer than fifty feet? Seriously, in a town the size of Whitehorse with only one grocery store, one post office, one damned theater?

Grabbing up the paperwork, he tore it into a hundred pieces and threw it in the air like confetti. He felt a little better.

His cell phone rang. For just an instant, he thought it might be Abby calling to say she'd changed her mind. All the other times they'd had problems she'd come back.

But it was only his father calling. He swore and picked up. "What?"

"I see your mood hasn't improved."

"Her car is gone. You think she came out and picked it up?"

"The sheriff sent two deputies out to bring it back to the office, where Ledger McGraw picked it up with one of his ranch hands."

Wade let out a string of curses. "I want to get out of this damned town."

"Oh, come on, don't you want a little retribution first? Have you forgotten? We have an ace in the hole, remember? We're in the catbird seat, son. Soon we will be calling the shots."

When his father had come to him with his plan, he'd thought the old man had lost his mind.

"You're going to get us both sent to prison. This can't possibly work."

His father had winked at him. "These years as a deputy, I've made a few…friends. Leave it to me. We can pull this off."

Wade had been skeptical at best. But to his amazement, the plan seemed to actually be working.

"So knock off the 'poor me' routine," Huck said. "Soon you will have the money to go anywhere you want. And we'll have gotten some retribution along the way."

"I HAVE GOOD NEWS," Travers said when he saw Vance.

He could use some good news. "How is that?"

"I'm calling a press conference tomorrow to introduce you to the world and announce that my son has been found."

This was not what he'd consider good news. Especially when Abby Pierce was upstairs, no doubt racking her brain to remember where she'd last seen him. "Do we have to?"

Travers put a hand on his shoulder. Vance tried not to flinch. He'd known all of this would feel... strange. A father he'd never known. A family he'd never met. A new name. He wondered if he was up to it. The money, the name that carried weight, the ranch and all the expensive horses, all that he could get used to. But the rest...

"Son, I want to introduce you to the world as a McGraw. I've waited twenty-five years. Can you indulge an old man?"

How could he not? "I understand, but I've never been good at getting up in front of people like that."

"It will be fine. You won't be required to say but a few words. Or none if you aren't comfortable."

Just stand there and smile into the cameras and let everyone speculate on me, he thought. "You're planning to tell the circumstances of how I was adopted."

Travers nodded. "I hope you don't mind. I think it might also help bring back our Jesse Rose."

Jesse Rose. His fraternal twin sister. He'd almost forgotten about her. Why not? Pretty soon they would be just one big happy family. Right, he thought.

"If I can help bring her home, of course I'll do it," Vance said, knowing he had no choice. He was Oakley McGraw. He needed to start acting like him.

For a moment, he forgot about Abby Pierce. "There is one thing, though," he said as Travers started to step away. "What do I wear for this…press conference?"

"I'm sorry. I should have thought of that. You'll want to pick up a few things. We can go into town—"

"Would you mind if I did this alone? I feel enough like a kid as it is."

"Of course you do. How foolish of me. Take one of the ranch pickups. There are keys on the board by the back door. I'll call the clothing store in town and tell them to put it on my account. Get whatever you need." He smiled. "Treat yourself, please. Head to toe. You're Oakley McGraw. Nothing is out of your reach." He started to turn away. "There is one more thing. Your mother. You know she hasn't been well. But she is doing much better. In fact, she wants to see you."

All Vance could do was nod as he thought, *Holy crap! Just when I think it can't get any worse.*

LEDGER TOOK THE stairs two at a time, anxious to see Abby. He'd picked up what she'd asked for from her apartment. It wasn't much. He'd been shocked to see how little she owned.

He tapped at her bedroom door. No answer. He tapped again and tried the knob. She stood at the window, her back to him, hugging herself as if cold.

"Abby?"

Startled, she turned from the window, looking scared.

"I knocked. You didn't hear. What is it?" he asked as she quickly rushed to him and threw herself into his arms.

"I was so worried about you," she said into his chest. "I thought—"

"I'm sorry. I hurried as fast as I could." He stared at her. "You're as white as a ghost. Are you feeling worse?"

She lifted her head to look up at him. "I don't know." He could see the fear still in her eyes. "I think I might be losing my mind."

"Why? What happened? Wade hasn't come here, has he?" He held her at arm's length to look into her beautiful face. It was still bruised. Every time he saw it, he felt anger boil up inside him. It was all he could do not to go after Wade.

Abby shook her head. "I saw someone in the hallway." He frowned. "A man. He came out of a room down the hall. When I saw him—" She shuddered and he pulled her close again.

"Are you talking about Vance? Vance Elliot. He's staying here. Abby, I'm sorry. There's been so much going on. I thought you knew. My brother, the one who was kidnapped… He's been found."

Her eyes were wide with horror. "*He's* the missing twin? He can't be your brother." She sounded as scared as she looked.

He drew even farther back to look at her. "Why would you say that?"

She pulled away to pace the floor. "When I saw him, I recognized him. And he recognized me. I had this jolt of memory, nothing I could recall, really, just this frightened feeling."

Ledger didn't know what to say at first. "You say

you recognized him? Could it be from the café in town?"

Abby shook her head. "It wasn't in that context. It was…a bad memory. I know that doesn't make any sense. It's just this…feeling more than a memory. But I know I've seen him before, and wherever it was, it wasn't…good."

"Okay," he said, wondering what to make of this. "And you say he recognized you? Did he call you by name?"

"No. He seemed as shocked to see me here as I was him. I made him nervous."

Ledger took this all in.

"I know I sound crazy," she said, stopping her pacing to step to him again. "I'm trying to remember where I saw him. So much of the past is a blank because of the concussions. I'm afraid I won't remember."

He held her, drawing her close and kissing the top of her head. "It's going to be all right. You're here." But so was Vance Elliot—soon to be Oakley McGraw, if his father had anything to do with it. He wondered how much he should worry. Wade had scrambled Abby's brain. Could he trust this feeling she had? Could he *not* trust it?

ABBY LEANED INTO Ledger's hard body. Breathing in his scent, she felt safe and loved in his warm, strong embrace. With his arms around her, she believed anything was possible. Even the two of them having a happy ending. She never wanted him to let her go.

But she couldn't shake off the bad feeling she'd had the moment she'd seen Vance Elliot in the hallway. Something was terribly wrong. If only she could remember where she'd seen him.

"Maybe I really am crazy."

"You're not crazy," he said, a smile in his voice. "You're going to be fine."

In his arms, she believed it. But when she was alone with her black hole of a memory… "I don't know." She stepped away to move to the window overlooking the ranch. She loved this view. It was so peaceful, unlike her mind right now. "Maybe my head is so jumbled up that I might never straighten it out again."

"The doctor said to give it time. You've been through so much," he said, stepping to her and clasping both shoulders in his big hands. His fingers tightened as if he was thinking of Wade. "Trying too hard to remember is only going to make your headache worse."

She nodded. "Thank you for not going after Wade."

His smile was tight. "You don't know what you're asking. You realize that, don't you?"

"Yes. I don't want you to lower yourself to his level."

Ledger let go of her. His laugh held no humor. "Oh, Abby, you don't realize how much pleasure it would give me to beat that man to within an inch of his life. I want to give him some of his own medicine." He smiled. "But for you, I won't go after him. All bets are off, though, if he shows up here."

She smiled and nodded through fresh tears. "Once this is over," she whispered as he took her in his arms. "Once this is over." But would it ever be over?

VANCE COULDN'T BELIEVE it as he sat behind the wheel of the ranch truck and looked at the fancy clothing-store bags and boxes piled high on the other side of the pickup.

"Treat yourself. From head to toe." That was what Travers—his father—had said. That meant Stetsons to boots. Any other time, he would have been over-the-moon excited. The truck smelled like good leather and expensive fabrics. It smelled better than anything he could remember.

As he looked down at his boots, he felt for the first time like Oakley McGraw. He'd never owned a good pair of boots before. Somehow it made him feel better about himself. At least temporarily.

He pulled out the burner cell phone, sick at heart

that he had to make this call now, of all times. But he didn't know when he was going to be able to get back into Whitehorse alone.

It rang three times before a male voice answered with "You done good, boy."

"Yeah," he said, loving the feel of the fine leather on his feet as much as the new gray Stetson perched on his head. For a moment, he thought about hanging up, starting the engine and seeing how far he could get away before someone came after him.

He didn't want to give any of this up, let alone have it snatched from him. He liked being Oakley McGraw, but it would be hard to get rid of Vance Elliot after twenty-five years of him living in the man's body. As Vance, he'd made his share of mistakes that were bound to come out.

But he had a more immediate problem. "The thing is—"

"What's wrong?"

"Abby Pierce. I crossed paths with her in the house today. She recognized me, but I could tell she was having trouble remembering where she'd seen me. But I have to tell you, that look she got in her eyes… It won't take her long to put it together."

"Where are you?"

"In town. Travers treated me to some clothing. He's planning on a big press conference tomorrow to tell the world that I am his son. But if she remembers before that—"

"Meet me at the Sleeping Buffalo rocks. Fifteen minutes."

"I'M GOING TO see your mother," Travers said when Ledger came downstairs. "I was hoping you and your brothers would come, as well."

"Sure." He'd been once when he was younger. He hated seeing his mother like that, and his father had said that he didn't want his sons going if it upset them. Cull was the only son who continued to visit her—not that she'd noticed.

"I heard she's doing better," Boone said as they started toward the front door for the drive to the mental hospital.

"She is," their father said, smiling. He looked so much happier now. His prayers had been answered. Now, if Jesse Rose would turn up... "She asked about each of you the last time I saw her."

"She's talking?" Ledger said.

"She is. Not a lot, but she's improved so much I have hope, and so do the doctors, that she could make a full recovery," Travers said.

On the drive to the hospital, they talked about the ranch, the horses and finally Vance.

"Is this press conference really necessary?" Boone

asked. "Yesterday, I was out in the pasture and a drone flew over low with a video camera attached to it. Is it ever going to stop?"

"Not for a while," Travers said as Cull drove. "When Jesse Rose is found, we'll have to go through it all over again, but eventually we'll be old news."

"That day can't come soon enough," Ledger agreed.

"If it ever does," Cull said. "Whenever our name comes up, it's in connection with the kidnapping."

"And Nikki's book on it isn't going to help," Boone said.

Cull shook his head. "I disagree. We're in the public eye. People want the inside scoop. Well, they will get it in the book. After that there won't be anything to add."

"I hope you're right," Ledger said. "I want to marry Abby, but I don't want to bring her into all this."

"Patricia still has to go to trial," Boone said. "Who knows how long it could take to find Jesse Rose, if ever. I can't see this ending for years, so unless you want to make the mistake of putting off your marriage again—"

"Abby isn't even divorced from her current husband," Cull pointed out. "I think we should just be glad that Oakley has been found."

"Yes," their father said. "Let's count our blessings. After the press conference tomorrow, I have a good feeling about Jesse Rose being found, as well."

Chapter Twelve

"Well, would you look at this dude," Deputy Huck Pierce said as Vance Elliot climbed out of the Mc-Graw ranch pickup. "Oakley McGraw, all duded out. How ya likin' livin' in luxury?"

All the way out to the Sleeping Buffalo rocks, Vance had been thinking he should just take off. It wasn't like he'd left anything he wanted back at the ranch. And he knew Travers McGraw would never send the cops after him. Not his own son. He could just keep going.

The problem was that he would eventually run out of gas. He didn't have a dime to his name. But as Oakley McGraw, he could have it all. It meant staying, though, and taking his chances with Abby remembering where she'd seen him. It also meant dealing with Huck and his son, Wade, he thought with a groan as he glanced past the two deputies to the rocks.

"So what's this?" he asked, motioning to two brown

boulders, a large one and a smaller one, under a roofed-over enclosure beside Highway 2. He was stalling for time and he knew it. As he stepped closer to the rocks, he saw that they appeared to be covered with tobacco and some loose cigarettes that had been broken and spread over the larger of the rocks.

"You ain't heard the story of the sleeping buffalo?" Huck asked. "These rocks are sacred. Indians—excuse me—Native Americans believe it has spiritual power. You see, the Native Americans were looking for buffalo, hadn't seen any and were worried. Then they saw what they believed was the leader of a herd perched high atop a windswept ridge overlooking Cree Crossing on the Milk River not far from here. It turned out just to be these rocks. But past it was a herd of buffalo. So they believe these rocks led them to the buffalo and that the rocks have some kind of special powers. That's why they leave tobacco on the rocks to honor the spirits."

"And you believe that?" Vance asked.

"You might, too, if you knew what happened back in the 1930s when the rocks were moved into town," Wade said. "Town folk swore that the rocks changed positions and bellowed in the night. So they hurried up and brought them back out here."

"No kidding?" Vance said, staring at the rocks. The larger one was way too huge for even a group of men in town to move by hand each night in order to scare people. He thought maybe there was something to the story since apparently a lot of the Native Americans believed in these rocks.

He wished he believed in something right now as he saw Huck fidgeting. He had something on his mind and Vance feared he wasn't going to like it.

"There's a hot springs up the road here, if you ever get out this way again," Wade was saying.

"Are we through shooting the breeze, because I want to know how things are going out at the ranch," Huck said impatiently.

Vance took a breath. He thought of his beautiful accommodations. He was now living in the lap of luxury—just as Huck had said—and he loved it. He'd never thought it would go this far. But now that he was so close to legally being Oakley McGraw, he didn't want it to end.

"There could be a problem," he said, turning away from the rocks. The sun beat down on him. Standing here, he could see the prairie stretched out in front of him for miles. This country was so open. He thought a man could get lost in it and thought he might have to before this was over.

"A *problem*?" Huck repeated, already looking angry.

He glanced at Wade. "It's your wife. I didn't realize that she was at the ranch because she's been holed up in a room down the hall. Well, I saw her today. And she saw me. I think she recognized me from that first night we met."

WATERS LOOKED AT the messages on his phone. Patricia. One of them caught his eye.

Travers came by to visit me.

He stared at the screen and swore. The last thing he wanted was for Travers to be talking to Patricia. Who knew what lies she'd tell him. She was determined to take Waters down with her. He didn't know how to stop her. Surely the sheriff and Travers knew that she was a liar.

But some things would have a ring of truth in them. He'd been so sure everything would be blamed on Patricia's conspirator, Blake Ryan. Blake had been the former ranch manager, an old family friend and one of Patricia's lovers. He would have done anything for Patty—and did.

Now, though, there seemed to be fallout around the case and Waters knew he was directly in the line of fire if Patricia kept shooting off her mouth. Plus, she said she had evidence in emails and texts.

He paced around his small apartment, telling himself that now would be the perfect time to leave the country. Except that what money he'd managed to put away over the years was in stocks and bonds and not that easy to liquidate. Also it was the worst possible time.

But if he could get his hands on some money...

"Calm down." He stopped pacing, tried to stop panicking. Vance Elliot was Oakley. He'd brought him to Travers. Everything was fine. Travers wouldn't take Patricia's word over his. If he could just hang in...

A thought struck him. If he could find Jesse Rose, Travers would be indebted to him forever. He thought about the strange call he'd gotten from that private investigator in Butte. Probably a dead end. But maybe he should mention it to Travers. Maybe make more out of it than it had been.

"WHAT THE HELL are you talking about?" Huck demanded. "I know Abby can't hardly remember her own name. That's right—not only do I have friends at the lab in town, but also I have friends at the doctor's office and in other places. She doesn't remember *anything*."

"Maybe," Vance said skeptically. "But if you had seen the way she looked at me."

Huck waved it off. "You're just being paranoid. Suck it up. So how are things going with Travers McGraw?"

"Like I told you, he's scheduled a press conference tomorrow to announce to the world that I am Oakley McGraw. After that, he wants me to change my name legally."

Huck burst out a huge laugh and pounded Vance on the back. "Nice work. I can see that you're enjoying the fruits of our labor. The accommodations up to your standards?"

"It's nice living out there."

Wade snorted. "I'll just bet. Abby eating it up?"

"She doesn't look good. I mean, she's still hurt pretty bad," Vance said. "She's kind of limping, holding her ribs, and there's bruises." He could see that this pleased both men. What had he gotten himself involved in? As if he hadn't known right from the get-go.

"So you stand up there tomorrow at the press conference," Huck said. "You tell the world how happy you are to be back in the bosom of your family and you start going by Oakley."

"What about the reward money? You said I'd get my share."

Huck's gaze narrowed. "You wouldn't be thinking about taking off once you got a little money in your pocket, would you?"

Vance looked away.

"Listen to me," the deputy said, closing the space between them. "This is for the long haul, not for a measly five hundred grand. You'll get your share but not until you are settled in and Daddy's put you in his will."

He blinked. "Why would you care about the will?"

"You let me worry about that," Huck said, patting him heavily on the shoulder. "I'll let you know when we're through doing business. In the meantime, stay clear of Abby. She's probably picking up on your nervousness. We're home free."

Vance could see now how this was going to go. At first it had been about the reward money. They were to split it and then part ways. But Huck was getting greedy. Which meant the deputies would bleed him dry for years if Vance let them.

LEDGER WAS STILL shaken from seeing his mother. He hadn't seen her since he was a boy. It had been shocking then. It was still shocking. Cull had gone to visit her at the mental institution over the years, but he and Boone had gone only once when she'd first been admitted.

He'd asked about her, though, when Cull had returned from a visit. "She's still catatonic. In other words, she doesn't know anyone, doesn't talk, doesn't respond to anyone around her," Cull had said. "She just sits in a rocking chair and...rocks."

Ledger had kept the rumors going around school about her over the years to himself. He didn't want his brothers or his father to know what the kids were saying about his mother.

"She's crazy scary. The nurses are all afraid of her."

"Her hair turned white overnight. She turned into a witch and puts spells on people."

"She sits and rocks and holds two old dirty dolls. She thinks they're the twins she kidnapped."

That was the hardest part, everyone believing his mother had helped kidnap her own children. Unfortunately, none of them still knew who inside the house had handed out the twins to the kidnapper on the ladder outside the window. The ladder had been found leaning against the house—one of the rungs broken halfway down. That had led the FBI and sheriff at the time to speculate that the kidnapper could have fallen with the twins and that the six-month-old babies had died.

Fortunately, they'd found out that that wasn't true.

Now Ledger stared at the white-haired woman in the rocking chair on the criminally insane wing of the mental hospital and wondered what *was* true. The woman in the rocker looked much older than fifty-seven—until he looked into her green eyes. There was intelligence there—and a whole lot of pain.

"Ledger," she said and held out her arms.

He stepped into them, kneeling down so she could hug him, and felt his heart break for all that she'd lost. Twenty-five years. Gone. Worse, only one of the twins had been found. If Vance really was the lost twin.

Ledger couldn't help thinking about what Abby had told him. Maybe it was just wires crossed in her brain. Or maybe not.

Worse, his mother was still a suspect in the kidnapping. But he didn't want to believe it. This woman who'd suffered so much... She couldn't have been responsible for helping the kidnapper take her own children.

"I want to see Oakley," his mother said as she looked at Travers. "Will you bring him to visit me soon?"

Travers promised he would. "He seems to have taken after you."

WADE WATCHED VANCE drive away. "We can't trust him."

Huck laughed. "You're smarter than you look. He's not going anywhere until he gets money."

"What if Travers gives him some?"

"He won't for a while. McGraw is no fool. He can see that Vance isn't comfortable in Oakley's clothes." Huck scratched his jaw, laughing at his own joke. "McGraw will spoon it out slowly to him so as not to scare him. Anyone can see that Vance has never had much. He won't want to overwhelm his son."

Wade had to hand it to his father. That night when he'd shown up with this crazy plan, Wade had been outside the garage putting new spark plugs in his old pickup. The moment he'd seen his father's face, he'd known something was up. He knew about the marijuana deal the old man had going on with Abby's mother, but he wanted nothing to do with it.

"Abby gets wind of this and she'll flip out," Wade had warned his father. "You're going to screw up my marriage."

"On the contrary, I'm helping you out. She'd never rat out her mother. This way we have leverage. One day, maybe you'll be as smart as me—probably not, but keep trying." He'd cuffed him and then changed the subject.

So that night when he'd seen the smug look on Huck's face, he'd thought, *Oh, hell, now what*.

"Somethin' I wanna show ya," his father had said. Wade had caught the smell of beer on the old man's breath even though he was still in uniform. Often he worried that Huck would get them both fired.

That was when he noticed the paper sack his father was carrying. Huck motioned for him to step into the garage. "Where's your wife?"

"In the kitchen making supper. Why?"

"Look at this." His father had opened the top of the large paper sack.

"What's that?" Wade asked after getting a glimpse of what appeared to be a stuffed toy horse.

"That is money, son." Huck had gone on to explain how he'd been one of the first law officers called out to the McGraw ranch the night of the kidnapping and how he'd found the stuffed animal lying on the ground and picked it up. "I was thinking eBay. People will pay a bunch of money for something from a crime scene."

Wade had interrupted to tell him what a dumb idea that was. "They'd have traced it back to you. They'd fire you, charge you with…tampering with evidence at a crime scene and who knows what else."

"Settle down," his father had said. "I put it away, all right, and forgot about it until I ran into this guy at the bar down in Billings. It was his blue eyes. Dark hair, too. I thought, hell, that kid could be the missing McGraw twin." Huck had started laughing. "We got to talking and…" He'd motioned to his pickup parked behind Wade's. The passenger side door had opened and out stepped Vance Elliot.

Wade had argued that it would never work. "They'll want a DNA test."

"Already got that covered. There's this cute little redheaded lab tech…" Huck had winked. "It gets better. Vance is adopted. No kidding. Tell me this couldn't be more perfect. And he's about the right age."

"But won't there be paperwork?" Wade had argued.

"Falsified to cover up the fact that his parents had knowingly adopted the son from what is now a famous kidnapping."

"But what if the real Oakley comes forward?"

"Who will believe him once our boy is in the big house on the ranch?" Huck had scoffed that things could go very wrong. "Five-hundred-thousand-dollar reward. Vance here gets a cut, but he will have the McGraw horse ranch."

"Along with his three brothers and his sister, if she turns up," Wade had pointed out.

"Stop looking for trouble," his father had said irritably. "This is going to work. Trust your old man."

That was when Wade had heard a sound from behind him. He'd turned in time to see the door to the kitchen close quietly.

Chapter Thirteen

Waters couldn't help looking at his watch. Vance was late for dinner. He saw that Travers looked worried.

"Where is Vance?" Boone asked as Travers finally told the cook she could go ahead and serve the meal.

"He went into town to get a few things to wear," Travers said. "I wanted him to look nice for the press conference tomorrow."

"You're really going through with this," Boone said.

"Of course. He's my son. I want the world to know."

"Also it won't hurt to get the kind of publicity we need for Jesse Rose to see it and possibly come forward," Waters interjected.

Travers actually shot him a smile. "Exactly. I have faith that both of the twins will have been found by the end of the year."

Louise was serving the salads when Vance hurried in.

"Sorry I'm late. Getting clothing took longer than I thought."

Travers seemed to light up as the young man came into the dining room. Waters saw that his other sons noticed. Nothing like sibling rivalry. But he wondered how long it would be before the new rubbed off Vance and Travers wasn't quite so enamored with his long-lost now-found son.

"Did it go well?" Travers wanted to know.

"I took your advice and let the clerk help me," Vance said, taking his usual seat next to his father. "I hope she didn't go overboard."

Travers laughed. "Not to worry. I just want you to have what you need."

Waters had been watching Vance and now saw him look around the table—and start. His gaze had fallen on Abby Pierce. She paled as the two met gazes across the expanse of the table.

"This is Abby," Ledger said as he, too, had noticed the exchange between his girlfriend and Vance. "Abby, I don't think you have officially met my... brother Vance. Or is it Oakley now?"

"Vance for now." The words seemed to get caught in his throat.

"But soon to be Oakley," Travers said, sounding pleased. "Unless you've changed your mind."

Vance looked again in his direction. "No, of course not. It will just take a little getting used to."

Waters noticed that Abby was still staring at the man as if trying to place him. He fought back the bad feeling that now knocked around in his chest. Things had been going so well. Except for Patricia. He and Travers had talked and now he would be handling some of the family affairs again. And he'd been invited to dinner almost every night since finding Vance.

He had his foot in the door. The last thing he wanted was for a problem to come up involving the soon-to-be Oakley. And yet, as he picked up his salad fork, he realized he'd been waiting for the other shoe to drop as if he was afraid to trust his good luck in Oakley turning up.

VANCE DIDN'T THINK he could eat a bite. He was still shaken from his meeting with the deputies. Huck scared him since he seemed to be carrying a grudge against the McGraws. His son, Wade, had mentioned something once about Huck having dated Travers's first wife, Marianne.

It must have been a long time ago since the

woman had been locked up in a mental ward for the past twenty-five years.

"I think after dinner, Oakley and I are going to go out and visit his mother."

Vance didn't realize Travers meant him until he felt all eyes at the table on him. "Tonight?" His voice had risen too high.

"There's nothing to be concerned about," Travers said. "I'm sure you've heard stories, but Marianne is doing well now and she is very anxious to see you."

There was no way he was going to get out of seeing his mother. Not gracefully, anyway. So he smiled and nodded and took a bite of his salad. He could have been eating wood chips, for all he tasted.

With each bite, he could feel Abby's gaze on him, burning a hole in him headed straight for his soul. If he had one.

He hadn't taken Huck Pierce seriously the first time he'd met him in a bar down by Billings.

"I'm telling you, you're the spitting image of the McGraw boys," Huck had said, fueled by the half dozen beers he'd consumed. "I think you might be Oakley McGraw."

He hadn't known who Oakley McGraw was and said as much.

"It's the most famous kidnapping in the state of Montana. Where you been living, under a barrel?"

He hadn't taken offense because Huck had been paying for the drinks, so he'd listened as the man had filled him in. Two missing babies, a boy and a girl.

"They think they were adopted by well-meaning parents who kept it quiet," Huck had said.

Vance had felt a strange stir inside him. "*I* was adopted." He'd always been told that it was some teenager who couldn't raise him. But years later he'd heard that it was an aunt who'd dumped him off when he was a baby and his parents had finally had to adopt him.

His old man hadn't minded having a son around to help with the work on the dirt farm they had. Vance couldn't wait until he was eighteen to escape it. He'd taken off at sixteen and hadn't looked back. He'd heard, though, that both his parents had died in a gas leak at the house. The place had been mortgaged up to the rafters along with the land, so he hadn't gotten anything. He'd let the county bury them. They'd never liked him, anyway.

"Here's what I'm proposing," Huck had said that night at the bar. He'd spelled it out. Vance had said he'd have to think about it. "Doesn't look to me like you have much for prospects. Don't be a fool. This is too easy since I have something that was taken with the male twin the night of the kidnapping. Oh, don't give me that look. I didn't kidnap the kid. I was one of the first deputy sheriffs at the scene."

"You're a deputy sheriff?"

Huck had laughed. "You bet your sweet ass I am. You think about it. You call me tomorrow or forget it."

Vance hadn't been able to sleep that night. He'd looked up the kidnapping online. Huck had failed to mention that the McGraws raised horses. Vance had been making his living as a horse thief. He'd started to laugh until he saw something else Huck had failed to mention. The McGraws were rich.

He'd called the number the deputy sheriff had given him early the next morning. "This is crazy, but I'm in."

Huck had laughed. "You won't be sorry."

Now the meal ended too quickly. Travers got to his feet. "Let's go see your mother."

Vance rose. He shot a guarded look at Abby. She was putting the pieces together. He could see it in her eyes. How long before she figured it out and blew the whistle on the whole damned thing?

As he started to leave the dining room, he just wished she would do it now and save him the trip to the mental hospital to see his "mother."

"You okay?" Ledger asked Abby as he led her back to her bedroom. She looked pale and he could tell she was still a little unsteady on her feet.

"I know you don't want to hear this, but I've definitely seen Vance before. There's something wrong."

"Wrong how?" he asked as they reached her room. "You're sure he's Oakley?"

"He had the stuffed toy horse that belonged to Oakley. Also he passed the DNA test. It came back that he's Dad's son."

Abby sighed as she took a chair near the window. He took the other chair in the room. "I can't trust my memory or my instincts or..." She met his gaze. "But the feeling is *so* strong. I know him from somewhere and it's worrisome."

"It will come to you," he assured her even though he wasn't convinced. "Let your brain heal. I can tell you have a headache. Can I get you something?"

"No. When I take the pills the doctor prescribed I feel even more fuzzy. But I'm all right."

"You're telling me that you don't trust Vance," Ledger said.

"No."

"That's good enough for me. I'll keep an eye on him. In the meantime, I'm going to move into the bedroom next door. I don't like you being on this wing with him in case your...instincts are right." Ledger had been staying at his cabin on the ranch. She knew he'd been trying to give her space. As they both knew, she was still married to Wade.

She looked relieved, though, that he would be close at hand. It wasn't just that she didn't trust Vance. She was a little scared of him, as well.

"Thank you. I hope I'm wrong. Your father seems so happy to have him here. I hate to think what it will do to him if Vance isn't the person he believes him to be."

"That's just it. We know very little about him. Jim Waters did some checking and swears there is nothing to worry about. But I have my reservations, too. I do wonder how it will go with Mother."

THE SMELL HIT him first, then the noise of the mental hospital. Vance halted just inside the door, telling himself he couldn't do this.

"It's okay, son," Travers said. "Give it a minute. I'm sure this is hard for you, seeing your mother."

Vance wanted to laugh hysterically. The man had no idea. "There was this neighbor girl. She had to be…restrained. She ended up in a place like this. I visited her only once. I couldn't bear going there." He shuddered at the memory. Crazy Cathy—that was what the kids at school called her when they'd get a glimpse of her from the school bus. She would be tied up to the clothesline and she would run, her face stretched in a lopsided smile because she loved Vance—almost to death. She finally got sent away after she'd tried to kill him with a butcher knife one night after seeing him with another girl.

"I'm so sorry," Travers said. "This must be even more difficult for you. If you'd rather not right now…"

"No." He just wanted to get it over with. Trying to block out the sounds, the smells, the tension that sparked in the air like heat lightning, he walked down the hallway to be let into the violent wing. The sounds down here were worse—the crying, the screaming, the tormented shrieks that made goose bumps ripple across his skin.

A nurse opened the gate for them and led them down the hallway. Vance didn't look into the barred windows. He stared at the floor at his feet, telling himself he could do this, but feeling the weakness run like water through his veins.

His mother used to say that he wasn't strong. "We just need to toughen him up." Then she'd give him the worst chores she could find on the farm. The calluses he got were heart-deep and still rubbed him raw some days. He knew he wouldn't be here now if it wasn't for his childhood and that made him angry. His adoptive mother was right. He wasn't strong.

The nurse stopped at a door, used her key to open it and then told Travers she would be right outside the door if he needed her.

Heart in his throat, Vance followed him into the room and stopped dead.

The woman sitting in the rocking chair had lightning-white hair that hung around her shoulders like a shroud. But it was the face that froze his feet to the floor.

"Oakley?" the woman asked with a voice that cracked. She motioned for him to come closer.

It took every ounce of his courage to take that first step, let alone the second one, until he stood before her.

"Oakley?" she repeated, her green eyes narrowing.

He couldn't speak, could barely breathe. He swallowed, trying hard not to look into those eyes as if he might be looking into his own hell.

She reached for him before he could move. Her wrinkled hand caught his and held it like a vise as she dragged him closer. The green eyes widened in alarm and he felt a chill rocket through him.

Then the woman shoved him away and began to scream.

ABBY HADN'T BEEN able to sleep last night. Her mind had been alive with strange flashes that could be memory or could be her losing her sanity. Knowing that Ledger was in the next room hadn't helped. Several times she'd almost gotten up and gone to him.

But she'd known what would happen. She was still married. It didn't matter that it was a bad marriage. It didn't matter what Wade had done. She couldn't go to Ledger. Just the thought of him lying in his bed…

This morning she'd felt a little better.

"Stop trying so hard to remember," the doctor had said when he dropped by to check on her. "You will make yourself crazy. If your memory is going to come back, it will, and when you least expect it. Relax. Enjoy this beautiful place. In fact, I think you should get out of this room. Maybe sit by the pool."

Abby couldn't help herself. She could feel the memories just at the edge of her consciousness and she had the horrible feeling that it was imperative that she remember. And soon.

"I'll see that she takes it easy," Ledger had told the doctor after thanking him for driving out.

Abby had tried to relax as she and Ledger went out by the pool after breakfast. She'd been glad that breakfast was more casual, with everyone eating on their own in the large, warm kitchen. Boone and Cull had already gone to work in the barns and Travers was in his office, so she and Ledger had the kitchen to themselves since the cook had gone into town for more groceries.

She was glad that Ledger didn't mention marriage again. Right now, she couldn't think of the future. There was so much of the past missing in her memory. She had to deal with it first. Or maybe she was just afraid of rushing into another marriage for the wrong reasons. She knew Ledger wanted to save her from Wade. For so long, he'd been trying to get her to leave Wade. But was that enough to build a marriage on? Once she was divorced, would Ledger still want to marry her?

Her head hurt even thinking about it. She had too much to worry about, she realized.

Ledger seemed content to sit with her by the pool and talk about the horses and his family's plans for the ranch. She found herself smiling at him. He was a man with dreams. And she loved him so much it hurt.

"See that land on the mountainside over there?" He pointed toward a pine-studded hollow below a rock ridge. "That's mine. That's where I will build the house someday." His gaze shifted to hers and she saw so much promise in his eyes that she wanted to cry.

"It's beautiful."

"Like you," he said and reached over to take her hand.

She closed her eyes and told herself that everything was going to be all right. But deep inside she felt afraid. Wade and his father were up to something. Something she'd apparently overheard. They wouldn't trust that she might never remember. This wasn't over. Once she left here…

"Abby?" Ledger looked concerned.

She opened her eyes, realizing she'd been gripping his hand too hard. "I'm scared," she admitted. "I can't think about the future until I know what in my past has me so terrified."

Something moved past Ledger and she looked in that direction to see Vance. He saw her and quickly disappeared from view. The bad feeling washed over her, threatening to take her under.

Ledger followed her gaze. "You still think something is wrong, don't you?"

She nodded.

"My father said that the visit with our mother didn't go well. When she got a good look at him, she screamed. They had to sedate her. He's worried that this might have set her back. He can't bear that she might revert back into a catatonic state again."

Abby shivered at the news. "She must have sensed what I do about him."

"A BOOK?" WATERS COULDN'T believe what he was hearing as he stared through the scarred Plexiglas at Patricia. "You do realize that Nikki St. James is doing a book on the kidnapping."

"Nikki St. James wasn't there that night. I was," Patricia said into the phone at the jail. She gave him a smug look. "They're giving me enough money that it will pay for my decent lawyer. That's right. I'm going to get off, and when I do, they are going to start looking around for the person who really poisoned my husband."

He knew what she would be selling. The dirt on the McGraw family. The dirt on him, as well. "What is it you want?"

"*Now* you want to deal?" she asked, sweet enough to give him a toothache.

"Patty."

"Don't call me that."

"You don't want to hang out all your dirty laundry."

"Don't you mean your dirty laundry, Jimmy?"

"Think of Kitten."

"Oh, now you're going to show an interest in her?" Patricia snapped angrily.

She'd told him that Kitten was his, but he'd never been sure it was true given the way the woman lied. He had a feeling that she'd also told Blake Ryan, the former ranch manager, that Kitten was his. It would explain why Blake had done her bidding.

He lowered his voice. "You know why we had to keep this a secret."

"To protect your relationship with Travers. But look how that turned out. Unless you've managed to get back into his good graces." Her eyes lit. "Oh, you have! You…stinker you. You always land on your feet, don't you?" Her eyes narrowed. "Well, hang on for the ride of your life. I'm about to bring down your world and Travers's, too." With that, she slammed down the phone, rose and motioned to the guard that she was ready to go back to her cell.

VANCE COULDN'T HELP being rattled.

Travers had apologized at length for taking him to see his so-called mother. "I should never have taken you to see her so soon," he'd said on the ride home. "Marianne is just now recovering after all this time. This is all my fault. I'm so sorry."

"It's all right," he'd said. "Maybe I scared her." He hadn't scared her. He'd seen the look in the woman's eyes. She *knew*. Somehow she knew he wasn't her son.

"I think she was expecting to see you as a baby," Travers had said. "Or maybe it was just too much for her."

But Vance knew better and he feared Travers Mc-Graw was having his doubts. Just not enough doubts to stop all this craziness.

The press conference was a blur. He'd blinked into the flash of cameras, stepped up to the microphone to say how glad he was to have found his birth family and had then been ushered to the ranch Suburban as reporters shoved microphones at him and yelled questions.

He managed to escape after lunch, telling Travers he wanted to go for a ride and just digest everything that had been happening. He'd used the burner phone to call Huck, who'd been in a great mood.

"Saw you on the news! You looked real smart in those new clothes. Next step, legally becoming Oakley McGraw."

"We need to meet and talk."

Huck's good mood had evaporated in a snap of the fingers.

"Okay," Huck said when the three of them met, this time out by Nelson Reservoir in a stand of trees. "So Marianne freaked last night when Travers took you to see her. How did McGraw react?"

"He felt bad about taking me there, made excuses for Marianne, but I could tell he was shocked and taken aback. He has to be thinking she saw something he hadn't."

Huck waved a hand through the air. "It wasn't like she cried, 'This isn't my son!' Even if she had, she's…*sick*. So forget about it. You're still good as gold. McGraw wouldn't have gone through with the press conference if he had any doubts."

Vance raked a hand through his hair, his Stetson hanging from the fingers of his other hand. It was hot, but a breeze came off the water, and in the shade of the trees it wasn't too bad. But still he was sweating.

"I saw Abby looking at me again. Now she's got Ledger looking at me the same way."

Wade swore and kicked a rock into the water at the mention of Ledger's name.

"It's just a matter of time. I see her trying so hard to remember," Vance said, hating that he was whining. "She remembers just enough that she doesn't like me, doesn't trust me, and she's been bending Ledger's ear about me. How long before he goes to his father with this?"

"You just borrow trouble, don't you?" Huck demanded angrily. "She *hasn't* remembered. She isn't going to. What you need to do is dig in. Stop acting like a guest at the ranch. You need to go to work in the barns with your brothers."

Vance stared at him. How did he know…? "The cook? *Louise is spying on me?*"

Huck smiled. "I told you. I make friends easily. I know what is going on out there."

"I think Vance is right." Wade spoke up. "You know Abby. Once she gets her teeth into something…"

Huck swore.

"What are we going to do?" Wade cried. "Let me go get her. Once we have her back—"

"Don't be a fool."

But Vance could see that Huck was more worried than he let on.

"Okay, maybe it's time to take care of Abby." Huck turned to Vance. "Make it look like an accident."

"What?" He'd hoped he'd heard wrong, but one look at the deputy's face and he knew he hadn't. He took a step back. "I didn't sign on for murder."

Huck quickly closed the distance between them and got right into his face. "You signed on for whatever I tell you or you'll be meeting with your own accident. Is that understood?"

Vance's blood ran cold at the look in Huck's eyes. There was something bitter and heartless in that gaze. The deputy wasn't joking. Worse, he thought Huck was right about the places where he had "friends." He wouldn't look at the cook the same now that he knew Huck had her in his pocket.

"You are Oakley McGraw," Huck said, looking

less dangerous even though Vance knew he wasn't. "You will have a great life if you don't weaken now, you understand? Abby *can't* remember who you are because that will raise suspicion and involve Wade and me. So take care of it."

"But that still leaves Marianne," he said, hoping to find a way out of this.

Huck laid a hand on his shoulder and squeezed just hard enough to make his point. "Marianne is mentally unstable. We aren't worried about her, okay? Don't make me worry about you. You're in this up to your neck. Just remember this. You double-cross me and you won't live long enough to see prison."

Go to the sheriff. Confess everything. But even as he thought it, he knew Huck was right. The deputy had friends everywhere. Look how he'd managed to get the lab tests to appear that Vance was a McGraw. He must have gotten someone to get him DNA from one of the real sons. Or maybe the lab already had something of the twins from the kidnapping.

It didn't matter how Huck had pulled this fraud off. He had. And now he'd painted Vance into a corner. When had it gone from simply pretending to be Oakley McGraw to murder, though? Broke and now involved in fraud with a psychopath, he didn't see any way out of this but one. He had to kill Abby Pierce.

Chapter Fourteen

"You think he'll do it?" Wade asked after Vance had driven away.

"Nope," his father said. "He has it in him, but he's too gutless."

Wade shot his father a look. "But you made it sound as if you believed he would." He wasn't about to admit the sense of relief he'd felt. He still loved Abby. He figured he always would.

But that love came with such a sense of guilt over how he'd mistreated her it had turned into something hard as flint. In order to be rid of it, he had to be rid of Abby. Not that he wanted anyone else to have her.

"Son, if there is one thing I'm good at, it's reading people. Vance…well, he's damaged, no doubt about it. That's one reason why I knew he'd jump at the chance to be Oakley McGraw. But he's weak. I knew he'd never be able to go the distance."

"What the devil was the whole point of this, then?"

His father smiled. "Because we don't need it to. I've contacted Waters through a friend. He's taking care of getting us the reward money."

"But once they find out that Vance isn't Oakley—"

"That is never going to happen," Huck said with so much confidence that Wade wondered if the man had a screw loose. "By then anyone who could hurt us will be dead."

He stared at his father. "How—"

"You don't worry about that end of it. I have it all figured out. But first, we need to stop out by that rattlesnake nest in the Larb Hills." Huck grinned. "I brought along a couple of burlap bags. That wife of yours? You're not going to have to worry about her much longer. Neither is Vance."

WATERS COULD SEE his world exploding in front of his eyes. Patricia was the missile coming in hard and fast. He had to do damage control before she hit. But that meant telling Travers the truth. Well, at least enough of the truth to cover his behind. All he had going for him was the fact that Patricia didn't believe he would tell.

He found Travers in his office. "Do you have a minute?"

The older man looked up and waved him in.

"Boone tells me that you've had another inquiry that sounds like it might be legitimate."

Waters had forgotten about the call from the private investigator in Butte. "Yes, there was something about the call. I mentioned it to Boone."

"Did you get any specifics?"

"Not exactly, but by the questions the PI asked, I think he might have information about Jesse Rose."

Travers leaned back into his chair and motioned Waters to sit. "This is great news. We should get on this right away. I'll talk to Boone about following up on it."

"The PI was called out of town. He said he'd be back in a week or so. I was planning to go myself."

"I'd rather have Boone go," Travers said.

Waters figured the lead would take Boone nowhere. But he had to look as if he was trying to help find Jesse Rose. "There was something else." He stopped. His role in this house was tenuous at best after he'd sided with Patricia. Now he wasn't sure how his confession would go down. Travers could fire him and that would be that. He hesitated.

"Yes?"

"I need to tell you something. I should have a long time ago, but Patricia begged me not to and I foolishly listened to her."

"If you're going to tell me that you're possibly

her daughter's father, it isn't necessary. I've known all along."

Waters stared at him. "How—"

"I knew about the two of you before the kidnapping." Travers's gaze hardened. "I also knew about the two of you after I married Patty."

He didn't know what to say. *I'm sorry* didn't quite cut it. "I don't understand."

"Oh, I think you do. That old expression, keep your enemies close."

"You see me as your enemy?" That shocked him. He'd always thought that Travers trusted him, maybe even liked him. "If you knew, why didn't you say something?"

"I like to see how things play out. I was fine with you and Patty because I saw that she was using you the same way she was me. A leopard really can't change its spots."

He wasn't sure if Travers was referring to Patricia or to him. "She's doing a tell-all book to help pay for her lawyer's fees."

Travers nodded. "I heard."

"I can try to get an injunction to stop the book from ever being published if you—"

"Not necessary."

Waters couldn't help feeling confused. "But the bad press…"

Travers laughed. "Did you really think that would bother me? Jim, I believe you're the one who doesn't want to see Patty's book published. But I figure by then her trial will be over and the truth will have come out."

"The truth?" he asked.

Travers only smiled and said, "If that's all, please make sure Boone has all the information about this private investigator in Butte. I want him down there as soon as the man returns."

VANCE HAD NO idea how he was going to kill Abby and make it look like an accident. All the way back to the ranch, he cursed his luck. If he hadn't been in that bar in Billings, if he'd never met Huck Pierce, if he'd never gone along with this crazy idea for money...

Money was the root of all evil. If he had some right now, he'd be gone. He'd just disappear. Maybe go to South America. All he would need was a fake ID, and he'd heard that you could buy those if you knew the right people.

Except he didn't have money and he didn't know the right people. But Huck did. All this time, the cook had probably been watching him, reporting to the deputy that Vance was down at the pool or lying around the house.

Who knew how many other spies the man had at

the ranch, he thought, reminded of the ranch hands he occasionally saw when he was down at the pool. It wasn't like Huck to show all of his hand, so Vance figured there were others watching him—not to mention Travers and his sons. He felt like someone was always watching him, looking for a crack in the story he'd built, waiting for him to unravel and admit he wasn't Oakley McGraw.

The house was unusually quiet when he entered. He looked around. Travers's office was empty. He thought he heard the clatter of pots and pans in the kitchen, but no voices. Happy not to be forced to make polite conversation with anyone, he took the stairs two at a time, wanting only to get to his room and hide out for a while.

He was almost to the top of the stairs when suddenly Abby appeared. Seeing her when she was so much on his mind, he reared back in surprise. Her eyes widened in alarm as he lost his balance.

Vance groped for the handrail, but it was slick and he wasn't close enough to get a grip on the highly varnished wood. He teetered and then felt himself start to fall backward. The irony of it didn't escape him as his arms windmilled wildly to no avail.

SHOCKED BY WHAT was happening, Abby rushed down a couple of steps to reach for the man. His hand closed on her wrist. He flailed, still off balance. But he held tight as she tried to keep her balance.

In those frantic moments, she realized he was so much heavier than her that she wasn't going to be able to keep him from falling. And with his hand clutching her wrist, he was going to take her with him.

She felt her heels lift off the step. Her free hand grabbed the railing, but Vance's pull was too strong. She felt herself falling toward him.

Abby let out a cry as Vance jerked her arm hard, then let go. She was thrown toward the center of the stairway as his body was pushed toward the railing. Her gaze tumbled down the long stairway to the marble floor below. She waited for her life to pass before her eyes as she felt herself falling through nothing but air.

Below her, the front door opened and Ledger stepped through. Their eyes met, his rounding in horror. He shot forward as if he thought he'd be able to catch her before she hit the bottom and the hard unforgiving marble.

She closed her eyes as a scream escaped her lips. She'd come so close to being with Ledger, but now fate had stepped in to keep them apart forever.

LEDGER'S CRY OF alarm mixed with Abby's scream as she began to fall. He rushed toward the stairs, his gaze locked on Abby. He'd only reached the bottom step when Vance's free arm shot out, the other looped over the handrail in a death grip. He grabbed Abby at the last minute.

For a moment, it looked as if Vance couldn't hold them both on the stairway. Ledger saw the pain in his face, the exertion as he looped his free arm around her waist and pulled.

He hadn't known he was holding his breath until he saw Abby find footing on the stairs. Vance let go of the railing and sat down hard on the steps. All the color had drained from his face, and even from where he stood, Ledger could see that the man was sweating profusely.

Abby had sat down, too. She was crying softly and holding her ribs after her close call. If Vance hadn't grabbed her when he did… But what were the two of them doing on the stairs together?

"Are you all right?" Ledger said when he reached Abby. He fell to his knees in front of her.

"Vance saved my life," she said between sobs.

His gaze went to the man.

"It wasn't like that," Vance said. "I was coming up the stairs not paying attention."

"I startled him. He started to fall backward,"

Abby filled in as they both seemed to be trying to catch their breaths.

"She grabbed me, but I was so off balance..." Vance finished with a look of such regret as he rubbed his shoulder. "I could have killed her."

"But you didn't," Ledger said. "You saved her. Is your shoulder hurt?"

"I think I might have pulled something," Vance said.

"I'll call the doctor to look at it." Ledger touched Abby's face, pushed back a fallen lock of her hair and wiped away a tear. "I'll have him take a look at both of you. I thought we agreed you'd stay off the stairs?" he said to her, smiling with such gratitude that she was all right. When he'd first seen her... If Vance hadn't grabbed for her at his own peril...

"Believe me, I'll take the elevator from now on," she said and let him enclose her in his arms. Past her, Ledger studied Vance.

"You're a hero," he said to his brother. "Thank you."

Vance shook his head. "I'm far from a hero."

VANCE'S HEROISM WAS the talk of the dinner table that evening. He'd pulled a muscle in his shoulder and had to ice it. Abby's ribs were even more sore from his saving her, but now when she looked at him, it was with gratitude as if her earlier suspicions were gone.

He tried to breathe, but his shoulder hurt like hell, and all this talk of how amazing he was hurt even worse. He'd had a chance to let Abby tumble down the stairs and instead he'd saved her—after she'd tried to save him.

"Maybe you should both stay off those stairs," Travers joked. "Seriously, I've given all my other sons a piece of land for them to build on one day, if they can be talked into staying on the ranch."

The table had gone deathly silent.

A piece of land? Vance swallowed.

"We can look at a map of the ranch later if you'd like and you can pick out a section you might want," Travers was saying.

"That is very kind of you."

"Kind?" The man laughed. "Son, this is your birthright."

His birthright. He hung his head, muttering, "Thank you."

"Here's to your future," Travers said, lifting his wineglass. "May it be everything you've ever hoped for."

When he looked up to lift his glass, he saw the cook standing in the kitchen doorway looking right at him. His heart took off at a gallop. She would report all of this to Huck.

Vance took a sip of his wine and felt it instantly curdle in his stomach. His future was anything but bright.

Chapter Fifteen

Abby stood at the window looking out over the ranch. "I can't stay here," she said, more to herself than to Ledger as she shifted her gaze to him. She could see that he wanted to argue the point.

"You can't go back to your apartment. Not alone," he said.

She had a feeling that if she went back to her apartment—back to town—more of her memory would return. Travers was getting more attached to Vance. She'd heard Travers offer him a piece of land on the ranch. She knew that was a mistake. She just didn't know why.

"Wade doesn't know where my apartment is and there's the restraining order..."

Ledger cursed under his breath. "You aren't that naive. He's just waiting for you. And if you think a restraining order is going to stop him..."

"What about my job?"

"You don't have to work there anymore."

She shook her head. "Ledger, I enjoy my work. I miss the people. I miss feeling like there is a little normal in my life."

He sighed deeply, pain in his eyes. "What is it you're running from? Is it me?"

Abby quickly shook her head as she turned to him. "Never you. But I'm still married to Wade. I can't move on until I put that behind me."

He nodded. "You need time. I understand that."

"What will people think, my staying here with you?"

"Is that what you're worried about? What people will think?"

The moment she said it, she realized she sounded like her mother. The same mother who was growing pot in her root cellar, the same one who guilt-tripped her into staying in a bad marriage because it was to her benefit—not her daughter's.

Abby touched his cheek. "I want a fresh start."

"With me?" Ledger asked.

She smiled. "Oh, yes, with you. But I jumped into one marriage. I won't jump into another even with you."

He dragged her to him and kissed her. "I want you so badly."

"I feel the same way. It's been awful knowing you

are just in the next room. I can't tell you how I have fought the need to come to you."

He let her go as if he felt the chemistry that arced between them as strongly as she did. "I'll wait as long as it takes." He grinned. "I've waited this long."

She had to smile.

"But you have to know Wade isn't finished with you. A man like him? His pride will be hurt. He'll take it out on you and this time he'll probably kill you."

"I know." She hated that she sounded close to tears. She'd cried so much over all this. "How do I get him out of my life?"

Ledger shook his head. "I don't know. But I wish you would stay here until the divorce is finalized. Maybe by then he will have realized it's really over. Maybe he will move on."

She nodded, but she knew neither of them believed that. He reached for her again. The memory hit her so hard, she cried out, jerking back.

Ledger looked alarmed as if he thought he'd hurt her.

"I saw them!" The memory hung before her, crystal clear, before it flickered and died away as she

tried to see more. *"I know where I've seen Vance. It was at the house. He was with Wade and Huck."*

LEDGER DIDN'T KNOW what to make of what Abby had told him. He found his brother Cull downstairs and pulled him aside.

"Since the first time Abby saw Vance, she felt she'd seen him before, and wherever it was, it wasn't good."

Cull lifted a brow. "In other words, she just had a feeling about him."

"Something like that, only just now she remembered where she'd seen him. He'd been at her house talking with Wade and Huck."

"What?" Cull rubbed a hand over his face. "Okay, if this is true—"

"Why are you questioning it?"

"Because Abby's had two concussions in a row. Her memory isn't the most reliable. After what happened earlier today on the stairs… Then add to that, the garage at the house is supposedly where she fell and got her first concussion…"

Ledger could see his point. "What if it's a true memory, though? What would Vance have been doing with Wade and Huck Pierce?"

Cull frowned. "Nothing good. We were led to believe that he didn't know anyone around here."

"Exactly. You think we should tell Dad?" Ledger asked.

"No," his brother said quickly. "It will just upset him. And after everything that's happened, including Vance saving Abby yesterday on the stairs, I wouldn't suggest it. Anyway, if it's true and Vance denies it, it would be his word against Abby's."

Ledger nodded. "It could put her in danger if I'm right and the three of them are up to something other than the obvious."

"The obvious being that Vance isn't our brother," Cull finished for him. "Then how do you explain the DNA test?"

He felt a shiver race up his spine. "The day Vance was tested, Huck Pierce was in the lab. He was flirting with one of the techs."

"Interesting, but certainly not conclusive. We could do another test with another lab, I suppose," Cull said. "It would mean getting DNA from Vance. That shouldn't be too hard. We could have him tested against one of us."

Ledger smiled at his brother. He knew he could depend on Cull. Boone would have stormed upstairs and tried to throttle the truth out of Vance.

"This shouldn't be too hard," Cull said. "Let me handle it. In the meantime…"

"Right, just be cool."

WADE WATCHED HIS father storm up and down the floor, half expecting the floorboards to crack.

"He saved Abby! Saved her!" Huck roared. "Came out looking like a damned hero."

"Maybe that works to our benefit," Wade said when his father had calmed down a little.

Huck spun on him. *"What?"*

"When something happens to Abby, Vance will look innocent."

His father stopped pacing and stared at him. "You really aren't as stupid as you look."

"Thanks." Wade realized how sick he was of his father's belittling. He would be glad when they got the reward money. He was leaving town, putting all of this behind him for good. But then he thought of Abby. Did he really want her dead? No. Could he stop his father? It was too late for that, he feared.

Huck was muttering to himself as he paced again. "I think we need to step up the ending to all this."

Wade had no intention of being around to see whatever his father had planned. "When do we get the reward money?"

"My friend talked to the attorney. He offered

to cut a check today, but my friend insisted it be cash, saying he wasn't alone in finding Oakley, that the others want to remain anonymous. Jim Waters doesn't care. He said he'd get the money. Won't be long now," Huck said, smiling broadly.

His mood could go from happy to furious in less than a heartbeat. Wade realized his own wasn't much better. The sheriff had the gall to suggest he go to something called anger management. He'd been insulted at the time, but maybe once he was gone from here, he'd check into it.

"So what happens now?" Wade asked, not sure he wanted to know.

WATERS LOOKED AT the stack of bills inside his briefcase. Five hundred thousand dollars. Travers had been adamant about going ahead and paying the reward.

"Are you sure you don't want to wait a little longer?" Waters had asked. "Maybe run another DNA test." He knew it was the wrong thing to say. Voicing his suspicions wasn't doing him any good.

But he was still shaken. Travers had known about him and Patricia all along. He'd known and not said anything. As he'd said, he'd wanted to see how it all played out.

The only thing the man hadn't known was that he was being systematically poisoned.

"Just pay the reward, Jim. Oakley is home. Boone will check out this lead on Jesse Rose. I feel good about it. So I suppose we should discuss your... retirement."

That had been plain enough. But at least he could continue billing the bastard until then. And he would, he thought as he slammed the briefcase. First he would get rid of this money. He felt as if Travers was throwing it away, but what did he care?

Vance wasn't Oakley. Waters would bet his stock portfolio on it. He had no proof, just a gut feeling. The same gut feeling that told him Patricia was going to take him down with her.

He looked at the briefcase again. His passport was up to date. All he had to do was book a flight to anywhere there was no extradition. He could live comfortably on what was in that case—even if he couldn't get his money out of his retirement.

Waters let out a laugh. He didn't even think Travers would turn him in to the sheriff. Instead, he'd pony up another five hundred grand to pay the reward and keep his mouth shut.

With a start, Waters realized this was exactly what the cagey old fool hoped he would do. This was "kiss off" money. Travers expected him to run.

LEDGER FOUND HIS father in his office, but one look at him and he felt his heart break for him. "What's wrong?"

Travers looked up in surprise as if he hadn't heard his son come in. For a moment, he seemed at a loss for words. "It's your mother. She's doing...worse. I blame myself. I should never have taken Oakley out to see her. Of course she expected a six-month-old baby—not a grown man. The doctor said she's trapped in that night twenty-five years ago."

"It isn't your fault. She asked to see him. You couldn't keep him from her."

His father laid his head into his hands, elbows on his desk. This was the most distraught he'd seen him. For so long, the man had lived on hope that his kidnapped children would be found. Ledger suspected it wasn't going quite like he'd hoped.

"I'm sorry," Travers said, lifting his head. "You wanted to talk about something?"

Now that he was here, Ledger almost changed his mind. "I want to marry Abby."

His father chuckled. "Son, that's not news."

"I know. I never got over her."

"I blame myself for that, as well. I should have let you marry her when you wanted to. I can't believe what she's been through."

Ledger nodded. "But your advice was good. Abby

had a lot of pressure from her mother and Wade. Also she was lied to. I don't blame her for doubting me. I didn't handle things well."

"All water under the bridge."

"Yes. That's why I hope you don't mind her staying here a little longer."

"You know I don't. I just worry. She's still married to Wade."

"Yes, but not for long. She's filed for a separation. Unfortunately, she has to wait six months in Montana before she can file for the divorce. At least here at the ranch, she's safe. But I can't keep her locked up here for six months."

VANCE HELD THE phone away from his ear and looked toward the big house. He didn't think he could be seen from the shade of the trees where he stood. Nor did he think anyone was home. But Abby.

"Are you a complete idiot?" Huck demanded.

He didn't bother to answer.

"You could have finished it right there on the stairs."

"She saved my life. I would have fallen if she hadn't grabbed me."

The deputy let out a string of curses. "You sound like my addled son. Now you have a soft spot for the woman, too?"

"No." Actually, he was scared of her. He kept watching her, thinking she was going to remember. While she seemed less standoffish since their incident on the stairs, she still had that memory lodged somewhere in that head of hers. Once it came out…

He heard a vehicle coming up the road to the ranch. "I should go." He was hoping it was Travers back from town. His "father" had gone in to set up a bank account for him.

"I should have thought of it before," Travers had apologized. "A man needs a little spending money."

Vance wondered what his father thought was a little spending money. Hopefully enough so he could take off in one of the ranch trucks and never look back.

"Any word on the reward money?" he asked now into the phone.

"Not yet," Huck said.

A lie. Travers had told him that the reward was being paid today by special messenger. That had surprised him. He'd thought the lawyer, Waters, would be handling it and said as much to the man.

"Jim Waters is no longer in my employ," Travers had said.

That had surprised him even more. "I thought he was like family." At least, that was what Waters had told him once.

"Family," Travers had repeated. "It's odd what makes a family, don't you think? It isn't always blood. But even blood sometimes can't hold a family together. I think it's trust and love." The man had smiled. "One day my sons will all marry and our family will grow. I hope to see grandchildren before I die."

Vance had thought of Cull and Nikki. "I would think you'll be hearing wedding bells before you know it."

"Yes. I hope Jesse Rose is here to see it. This family won't be whole again until she's home. And her mother, too." Travers had brightened. "At least you're home."

"You still there?" Huck asked over the phone, sounding even more irritated.

"I'm here." Right here at home.

"Just do your job."

Vance disconnected and headed for the house. Once Travers handed him that checkbook… And yet as he walked up the back steps, he felt a pang. If only he truly was Oakley McGraw. Surprisingly it wasn't the ranch or the money or name that pulled at him. It was the idea of having a father like Travers McGraw.

Chapter Sixteen

"Here, let me help you with that," Ledger said as he saw the cook struggling with a large box. He'd been busy making him and Abby a picnic lunch. He planned to surprise her with a ride around the ranch.

The fiftysomething matronly woman had just come into the back door with the box and seemed anxious to put it down. But when he tried to take it, the cook turned away from him. "I have it," she said, sounding as if out of breath. "But thank you." She set it down carefully.

He noticed that the top had been taped closed and wondered idly what was inside that so much tape had been used. Live lobsters?

She turned, looking nervous, and he realized he was making her so. "Did you need something?"

"No—sorry." He tried to remember her name. Louise? Elise? Eloise? He couldn't be sure. They'd had the same cook from as far back as he could re-member. It was hard since they'd gone through a few before they'd gotten this one. Also he had the feeling that, like the others, she wouldn't be staying long. His family was a little too infamous and Patricia's arrest hadn't helped.

Ledger had forgotten why he'd come into the kitchen. His mind was on Abby, as usual. He'd real-ized that he couldn't keep her here like a prisoner. And yet he couldn't let her move back into town—not with Wade on the loose.

Now that she'd thought she remembered seeing Vance with Wade and Huck Pierce, he was all the more worried about her. He'd been so sure she was safe while in this house. But with Vance here, too…

Through the kitchen window, he saw Vance com-ing out of the trees at the back of the house. That was odd. He appeared to be pocketing a phone. Ledger realized he'd never seen Vance with a cell phone be-fore. Who had he been calling that he hadn't wanted to make the call in the house?

"If you'll excuse me, I have work to do," the cook said.

"Yes, of course," Ledger told her distractedly and put the box she'd left on the counter out of his mind as he heard the elevator. Abby.

"VANCE!"

He'd practically run into Travers as he'd come in the back door of the house.

"This is for you."

He took the envelope and glanced inside. The paperwork from the bank—along with what looked like a savings account bankbook and a checkbook. He wanted to see how much was in his account. The waiting was going to kill him.

"You need to sign some forms in there and return them to the bank," Travers was saying. "But you should be all set."

"Thank you so much," Vance said sincerely.

"You're my son."

He felt the warm, large hand on his shoulder and swallowed.

"But we do need to talk about getting your name changed legally—if that's still what you want. Also I hope you've been thinking about what section of land on the ranch you would like. I've hired a new attorney. I'd like to get this taken care of right away."

Vance could only nod.

"There is one other thing, though."

He froze. Why did he always expect the worst?

"I want you to pick out a horse. A man should have his own horse." Travers chuckled. "There's a few out there. You do ride, right?"

"Yes. As a matter of fact, I'd been wanting to saddle up and take a ride. I wasn't sure if that was all right."

Travers looked sorry again. "Son, this is your ranch, too. I want you to enjoy it. I also hope that you might be interested in working it with your brothers."

He'd known that was coming. "Absolutely. I just need to learn the ropes."

The man looked delighted. "I'll tell Cull. He'll get you started. Tomorrow is soon enough. You're settling in here all right?"

"I am."

"I know it will take a while for it to feel like home."

Vance held the manila envelope with the bank papers in it to his chest. "Yes, this is all so new for me." He couldn't wait to leave the room, feeling as if he'd won the lottery. Except he didn't know how much he'd won. Or worse, how long it would last.

LEDGER MET THE elevator as it came down, anxious to see Abby. Her injuries were healing and he knew it wouldn't be long and he'd have to let her go. That scared him in a way that nothing on this earth did. She would never be safe as long as Wade Pierce was out there.

As the door opened and he saw her, his heart did

a vault in his chest. He never saw her or heard her voice that it didn't send a thrill through him. He loved this woman. He'd never been able to let go because of it.

"Hey," he said, feeling like he'd been injected with helium.

She smiled broadly. She was almost her old self again. He could see it in her eyes. There was no reason for her to stay here—other than the fact that her husband was out there somewhere planning who knew what.

"I thought you might want to go for a ride. You've been cooped up too long. What do you say? Want to see my favorite parts of the ranch?"

"I'd love that, assuming you don't mean on a horse."

He laughed. "I'm not sure your ribs could take that. I've packed us a picnic."

"You think of everything," she said and squeezed his arm.

He wished he did think of everything. Otherwise, he would have better understood why Abby married Wade. If he'd known about the lies… As his father had said, "Water under the bridge." But still it was hard not to want to rewrite history and save them both a lot of pain.

As they started through the living room, he heard

a vehicle pull up out front, engine revved. Through the window, he saw nothing but a cloud of dust. Someone was in a hurry. His father and Cull came out of the office, both having heard the vehicle.

The knock at the door sounded urgent. Or angry. Just like the thunder of the boot heels did on the porch.

"I'll get it," Ledger said and then turned to Abby. "Wait here." He moved to the door, expecting it would be Wade.

Opening the door, he found a cowboy he'd never seen before standing there. He wore worn dirty jeans, a Western shirt with holes at the elbows and a belt with a rodeo buckle. The cowboy reached to take off his straw cowboy hat at the sound of the door opening.

Sans the hat, his dark hair caught the sunlight like a raven's wing. The young man brushed back a lock as he turned to look at him. Ledger found himself gazing into intense green eyes the same shade as his mother's. For a startled moment, Ledger thought he was seeing a male version of his mother.

"Can I help you?" he asked the man, his voice sounding calmer than he felt. There was something about this cowboy...

"No, but I can help you," the young man said, still

standing in the doorway. "I heard there's someone here claiming to be Oakley McGraw."

That didn't surprise Ledger after the press conference had gone viral. What did surprise him was that this cowboy had not just gotten onto the ranch, he was standing at their front door.

"And what does that have to do with you?" he asked.

"The name's Tough Crandall. Before you ask, my father rodeoed and so did his father, thus the name."

"Well, Mr. Crandall, I'm not sure what that has to do with my brother Oakley—"

"I've been out of state. I just happened to see on the news that the McGraw kidnapping son had been found. I'm here to tell you that Vance Elliot is not your brother."

"How would you know that?" Ledger demanded.

"What's the problem?" his father said, moving from where he and Cull had stopped just outside his office doorway.

"Mr. McGraw," Tough said to Travers, hat in his hand. "I heard you'd been sickly. I'm sorry to hear that. I didn't want to bother you, but I can't let you be tricked. The man staying with you pretending to be your son is a fraud."

"I think you'd better step inside," Ledger heard his

father say. He could tell by Travers's shocked look that he'd seen the cowboy's green eyes and dark hair.

Once inside the office, his father asked Tough Crandall to sit down. The cowboy looked around at the expensive furniture and said, "I'd prefer to keep standing if you don't mind. I picked up a couple of horses over in Minot earlier today. I would have waited and come after I'd cleaned up, but I was afraid it couldn't keep. Anyway, this won't take long."

"Mr. Crandall…" Travers began.

"Please, call me Tough."

"All right, Tough. Why is it you think Vance isn't Oakley?"

Tough looked down at his straw hat for a moment before glancing up again. Ledger saw the effect those green eyes had on not just his father but his brothers, as well. Even Boone, who had quietly joined them, was staring at the man.

"Because, sir, I'm your biological son."

Travers cocked his head. "And what makes you think that?"

"My mother told me all about my adoption. I've known since I was five."

"Then why didn't you come forward before this?" Cull demanded.

Tough chewed at his cheek for a moment. "Beg your pardon, but I had no good reason to. I have parents who raised me just fine and I didn't want to bring that kind of trouble down on them. They are good people who believed they were doing the best for me. I agree with them."

"Are you saying you didn't want to be a Mc-Graw?" Boone asked, sounding as if it wouldn't take much more to make him mad.

"No offense," Tough said quickly.

"Who did your mother say brought you to her when you were six months old?" Travers asked.

"Pearl Cavanaugh from the Whitehorse Sewing Circle. She, too, meant no harm. God rest her soul."

"Do you have any proof?" Boone asked.

"No, other than me standing here telling you what I know."

"But you'd be willing to take a DNA test?" Ledger asked.

"I didn't come here looking to be adopted into the family. I just thought you ought to know that Vance Elliot is an impostor."

"Vance passed the DNA test," Boone challenged.

Tough nodded as he seemed to study the lot of them. "Then you've got more vipers among you than even I thought." He took a step back. "I've done what I came to do. Believe me or not, doesn't matter to me. I just couldn't have this on my conscience without speaking up." He turned toward the door.

"Just a minute," Travers said. "My youngest son was taken from his crib with two items—"

"I saw that on the news," Tough said with a sigh. "I don't know anything about a stuffed toy horse. But I had a baby blanket with tiny horses on it. It was blue. The horses weren't quarter horses like you raise. They were Arabians. My mother gave me the blanket before she died. She told me to do with it what I wanted. I burned it."

A gasp came up from the room. "Why in the hell would you do that?" Boone demanded.

"Because I had no interest in doing what I'm doing right now," Tough snapped. "I won't be grilled. I won't be tested. I won't be looked at under a magnifying glass. I sure as hell don't want any press conference for the world to know. I *know* who I am, who my 'real' parents are, and I'm fine with that."

"But if you're Oakley—"

Tough cut Travers off. "Please, sir, don't make me sorry I came here. I couldn't let you be defrauded. But if you want to go on believing Vance Elliot is your son, that's fine with me. Please don't take offense, but I want no part of this family or what comes with it." He stuffed his straw hat onto his thick head of dark hair and lit out the door, leaving behind a stunned silence.

VANCE HAD WATCHED the whole thing from the doorway of the kitchen. After Abby had come down in the elevator, he'd gone into the kitchen and, finding it empty, had gotten himself a snack before opening the envelope.

Now he stepped back so no one saw him.

He heard a sound behind him and turned to see the cook. She had her phone in her hand. All the color had drained from her face.

She must have heard what was going on, as well. She was looking scared, no doubt because she'd been snitching to Huck about him. She was probably afraid she'd get drawn into all this.

"Please tell Mr. Travers that I'm not feeling well and have to go. I'm sorry about dinner." She headed for the door. He saw her glance at a large box sitting on the counter and she seemed to avoid it, increasing her speed as she went out the door. He noticed that some of the tape had been removed from the top of the box. There was a pair of kitchen shears next to it.

Whatever the cook had been getting out of the box, she seemed to have lost interest. Vance had the feeling that they wouldn't be seeing her again.

He wanted to run, too. He'd opened the envelope with his new bank account information but had seen right away that until he signed the necessary forms, he couldn't withdraw any of the ten grand Travers had put in his account. Ten grand. He'd had to count the numbers since he couldn't believe it. There was also a note in the envelope that read, "Thought you might want to buy yourself a vehicle. Let me know and I will see that the money is put into your account."

He'd groaned when he'd seen that. If he stayed, he got to buy himself a brand-new pickup. It was all too much. Worse, it was all a lie.

Had he really thought this was going to last? He couldn't stay. Even before that cowboy had shown up, he'd known that. But he also couldn't hide in the kitchen like the phony he was.

Vance walked into the living room, feeling the tension thick as fog. "The cook just told me to tell you that she isn't feeling well. She's sorry about dinner." He knew he couldn't ignore that tension. Or the way they all looked at him. "What's going on?"

"Some cowboy just stopped by claiming to be Oakley McGraw," Boone said. He was the most suspicious of the brothers. Vance couldn't tell who he thought was lying. Maybe both him and the cowboy.

"Well, he's too late, isn't he?" Cull went to the bar and poured himself a drink. The others joined him, all except Travers. "You passed the DNA test. You're Oakley, right?"

Vance swallowed, his throat too dry to speak. Anyway, what would he have said?

"That was disturbing," Travers said as he looked at his sons, his gaze finally taking in Vance.

He thought of how much he'd wanted this man to be his father. More than he'd wanted the money and the name. He felt an apology working its way up from deep in his chest.

His cell phone rang. He cursed silently. He'd stupidly forgotten to turn the darn thing off after his call to Huck. Pulling out the phone with trembling fingers, he looked at caller ID. *Huck.* It was marked Urgent.

He saw he'd missed an earlier text from Huck. It read: Unless you want to die, get out of the house. Now!

"I should take this." Quickly turning, he headed for the back door, wondering what this could be about.

Chapter Seventeen

"Did any of you know he had a cell phone?" Ledger asked the moment Vance was gone. Abby had sat down with the others. He joined her. She looked as shocked as he felt.

"Everyone in the civilized world has a cell phone," Boone snapped. "What is your point?"

"I just wonder who's calling him."

"You think he didn't have a life before he came here? Friends? People who care about him?" Travers asked as if he'd wondered the same thing.

They all looked after Vance for a moment before Cull spoke. "This Tough Crandall. He described the baby blanket perfectly. The type of horse on the blanket was never released."

"But he didn't have the toy stuffed horse," Ledger said.

"Vance did," their father said.

"For the sake of argument, let's say Tough Crandall

is Oakley," Cull said reasonably. "How is it he had the blanket but not the stuffed horse?"

Boone brought his drink over to the couch and sat down. "The stuffed toy was taken the night of the kidnapping along with Oakley and his blanket, right?"

"Maybe the kidnapper dropped it when the ladder rung broke," Cull said.

"And the kidnapper's accomplice picked it up?" Boone said.

Ledger felt a chill. "Or whoever was the first person on the scene."

"Like maybe one of the deputy sheriffs?" Abby said.

Travers sighed. "All this is just speculation. Vance's DNA matched."

"Dad, there's something I need to tell you," Cull said and looked at Ledger. "I've taken DNA from Vance's room and some of mine. I've had another test done at a different lab."

"Why would you do that?" His father sounded angry.

"Because Abby remembered something," Ledger said, looking at her. She nodded and he continued, "She remembered seeing Wade and his father with Vance. It was at her house."

"*What?*" Travers shook his head. "When was this?"

"Before he showed up at our door claiming to be Oakley. That's not all," Ledger continued. "When we were at the lab getting Vance's DNA test done, I saw Deputy Sheriff Huck Pierce talking to one of the lab techs."

The room went deathly quiet again.

"Let's all take it down a notch here," Travers said, but Ledger saw that he looked worried. "You realize what you're accusing Vance of being involved in."

"Fraud," Boone said, putting down his drink and getting to his feet. "I think someone should go check on Vance."

Ledger reached for Abby's hand. "We're going on a picnic. Hope you get it all worked out before we get back."

They'd barely reached the pickup when the back of the house exploded.

VANCE HAD REACHED the trees past the pool house and was about to put in a call to Huck when the world behind him went up in flames.

He spun around in horror as he looked at the back of the house. The kitchen wing looked leveled while the rest of the house was quickly catching fire.

For a moment he couldn't move. Two ranch hands came running from the direction of the barns. Out of the smoke at the back of the house, he saw Boone.

He'd been knocked to the ground but was now running back toward the burning house.

Vance's cell phone rang. Still in shock, he took the call.

"Did you get out in time?" Huck laughed.

"You did this?" he demanded.

"And just imagine what I will do if you cross me," the deputy said. "Now get rid of this phone. I'll find you when I need to talk to you again."

LEDGER GRABBED ABBY, not sure at first what had happened as glass showered over the porch as the front windows of the house were blown out.

The front door burst open. Cull and his father came stumbling out. "Call the fire department," Cull was yelling.

Ledger fumbled out his phone. Through the door he could see smoke billowing into the living room from what had been the kitchen.

He dialed 9-1-1 as he drew Abby farther away from the burning house.

"Are you all right?" he heard Cull ask his father. He noticed that the older man was holding his left shoulder.

"I'm fine. Go!" his father said as he stumbled toward one of the pickups parked out front.

Cull was running for their water truck parked next to one of the barns.

The 9-1-1 operator answered. Ledger quickly gave her the information, his mind reeling. What had happened?

"There was an explosion. The house is on fire."

"Is everyone all right?"

"I don't know," he said, suddenly terrified. Boone had started out the back door to go find Vance. The barns were far enough away that the ranch hands and the horses should be fine. But Boone...

"One of my brothers... I don't know where he is." And Vance. Ledger realized he'd never thought the man was his brother. "And another man."

"I'll send an ambulance, as well," the operator was saying. "The fire department is on its way."

HUCK HAD HEARD the call come over the radio and smiled. It just didn't get any better than this.

He drove partway out of town so he could see in the direction of the McGraw ranch. Black smoke billowed up into a cloudless blue sky.

With luck, Travers McGraw and at least some of his sons were dead, Abby along with them. If that damned cook had done her job, the box with the explosives in it would have been left under the front stairs, where it would have done the most damage.

Not that he'd told the woman what was in the box. He'd just told her to handle it with care and not say anything to anyone. It was a surprise.

Idly, he wondered if she'd been surprised.

You're a coldhearted bastard. He heard the last thing his ex-wife had said to him. "Yes, I am. Life made me that way."

And now he was getting back at everyone who'd wronged him. He had the five hundred thousand dollars from the reward coming. He'd give some of it to Wade and then he was gone. There was an island somewhere calling his name. Vance was now a Mc-Graw. He'd be fine. And if he didn't like getting ripped off on the reward money, what could he do about it, Huck thought with a laugh.

For a moment, he watched the smoke rising higher in the sky as flames consumed more of the McGraw house. Things would have been so different if Marianne had married him and not McGraw. He would have done anything for her. Hell, he had that scholarship to the university. He was going to be an engineer, maybe build dams or skyscrapers; he hadn't decided.

But when she'd married McGraw, he'd lost his drive. Nothing mattered. He'd married Wade's mother on the rebound and his life had gone downhill from there.

An ambulance had been sent out to the ranch since they were unsure how many people had been injured. Huck waited patiently for the news, telling himself even if McGraw wasn't dead, his house would be gone. He would have been hit where it hurt the most. The house McGraw had built for Marianne? Gone. Just as Marianne was gone in every sense of the word.

He thought about the twins. They, too, were gone. In the months since more information had come to light about what had been taken from the house the night of the kidnapping, Vance was the only one to come forward.

McGraw had lost Oakley and Jesse Rose. He'd lost Marianne. And now he'd lost his house and hopefully his life.

"Got you," Huck whispered as he watched the cloud of smoke grow larger and larger against the skyline.

VANCE STEPPED BACK into the trees as Boone yelled at the ranch hands to let all the horses out. The two headed for the barns, while Boone raced back into the burning house.

A few minutes later, horses came running out, wild-eyed in terror and headed out across the pasture away from the burning house.

Vance was too shocked to do more than stare at the flames licking wildly at the large house and try to make sense out of what had happened. What would happen now? Who had been killed? Would they think he had done this?

Since this was Huck's doing, Vance was in it up to his eyeballs. No one would believe he hadn't had something to do with this, even if they couldn't prove it.

Was that the way Huck had planned it? Was he going to let him take the fall for this? Was that why he'd texted him to get out?

Had the deputy already gotten the five-hundred-thousand-dollar reward money?

There was also the possibility that Huck warned him about the explosion hoping he would be the only one to survive and all this would be his so Huck could blackmail him right into his old age.

But what to do now?

If he was a real son, he'd be helping with the horses or running to the house to see if he could help who-ever was still inside.

But he wasn't and Tough Crandall's visit had raised enough doubt that this would soon be over. The sher-iff would be investigating. More DNA testing would be done and when he failed...

Vance began to run in the direction of the house

only to swerve at the last moment and race toward the front of the house and the pickups parked out there. If one of them had a key in it...

"HERE, TAKE MY father to my cabin up the road," Ledger said to Abby. "I have to help my brothers fight the fire until the rural fire department gets here." She started toward her rental car, but he handed her the keys to his pickup. "Take my truck. The road is rough. I'll have the EMTs come down there to look at his shoulder."

"I'm fine," Travers said. "We need to find your brother."

"Dad, I don't want to have to worry about you. Go with Abby. I'll do what I can here."

Abby could tell he didn't want his father watching the house he'd loved burn to the ground. She couldn't see how they could save it the way it had gone up in flames.

She was happy to help. Getting into the pickup, they started up the road when she had to pull over and let the fire trucks go by. She just prayed that Boone had gotten out.

Travers was looking back, tears in his eyes. "Still no word on Boone?" he asked. "Or...Vance?" She noticed he hadn't called him Oakley.

She shook her head. "I'm sure Ledger will call the minute he knows something."

Travers nodded and closed his eyes.

LEDGER WAS JUST about to go back inside to look for Boone when his brother came bursting out the front door in a cloud of smoke.

"Where is Dad?" Boone cried.

"He and Cull got out. Cull's gone to get the water truck. Abby and Dad are fine. I've sent them to my cabin. I didn't want Dad to see this. He's been through enough."

"What the hell happened?"

Ledger shook his head and called Abby to give her the news as his brother ran toward the second water truck. Cull was already watering down the closest barn. Clearly, he could see that it would be impossible to save the house without more resources.

At the sound of sirens, Ledger turned to see the fire trucks and ambulance in the distance.

VANCE CAME AROUND the side of the house as Ledger went to join his brothers to water down the barns. He rushed through the dark smoke toward the closest pickup. All he could think about was getting out of there. Let them think he died in the fire. It would be days before they realized his body wasn't in the ashes. Meanwhile, he would have put miles between him and this place.

No keys in the first pickup. Or the second. He swore. The smoke was starting to get to him. He spotted Abby's car and raced toward it. Behind him, the flames cracked and popped. Sparks flew into the air. The heat of the blaze felt as if it was frying his skin.

He could hear sirens and see the trucks coming up the road. He had to get out of there. If he stayed, he was looking at prison for a crime he didn't commit. He reached Abby's car, threw open the door and reached around the steering wheel, praying that the keys would be there.

They were!

His luck had changed. His mind was working again. If Huck had the reward money, he would get his share or blow the whistle on the deputy. Two could play at blackmail.

He dropped into the seat, reached for the key, turned it. The car engine caught and started. Vance glanced at the house, thinking what a waste and wondering who might still be inside.

He threw the car into Reverse, not letting his mind go there. He braked and looked again at the house, his senses warning him not to run. He would look even guiltier if he did. Maybe he could turn state's evidence on Wade and Huck. Maybe he could get out of this with a little honor.

He put the car in Park and turned off the engine, thinking about Travers McGraw and wishing with all his heart that he really had been his son. How different his life could have been.

Did he really think there was hope for him, that he could change? He told himself he needed to help water down the barns. He needed to be a different man, the kind of man Travers McGraw thought he'd welcomed into his family.

He reached for his door handle when he heard a noise. At first, it didn't register. A buzzing sound that he could barely hear over the roar of the fire.

Vance looked down at the floorboard, shocked to see what was coiled there. Two rattlesnakes intertwined, both of their ugly heads raised and looking right at him.

He jerked the door handle in that instant before the first one struck. He threw himself out of the car as the second one caught him in the neck. Its fangs going so deep that the snake was still clinging to him as he fell screaming from the car. He tore the snake from his neck.

Over the roar of the blaze, he heard the sirens. Looking up, he saw the first fire trucks pull up. He ran toward them, screaming for someone to help him as venom raced like flames through his veins.

WADE STARED AT his father, then at the cloud of smoke in the distance. "What did you do?"

"Instead of merely whining, I took care of your wife and her boyfriend," Huck snapped. "You should be thanking me. Hell, if it wasn't for me and Abby's mother, you would have never had Abby as long as you did."

"What are you talking about?" Wade demanded, his voice breaking.

"McGraw never had another girlfriend. He was in love with Abby and planning to marry her after college. And he would have if we hadn't tricked Abby into believing he was cheating on her. Why do you think she rushed into the marriage with you? You would never have stood a chance with her otherwise."

"You lousy son of a—" Filled with rage, he took a swing at his father. Huck easily stepped aside and hit him in the back of the neck. Wade staggered, turning to look back at his father. Lies, all lies. He felt as if his entire world had imploded.

He shook his head. He wanted to blame his father for all of it, but he couldn't. He'd gone along with this stupid plan. He could have walked away.

He could have gotten help. He could have been a decent husband.

"Where do you think you're going?" his father demanded as Wade turned and walked toward his pickup.

He didn't bother to answer as he climbed behind the wheel. He had to find out if Abby was still alive. He had to see her. Restraining order be damned.

"Don't go out there," Huck yelled after him as he took off in a cloud of dust and gravel. He roared out of Whitehorse. Smoke billowed up into Montana's big sky.

LEDGER AND HIS BROTHERS, along with the hired hands, managed to get the horses to safety and save the barns. Now, covered with soot, he stared at the ashes of the house. The firefighters hadn't been able to save it.

Smoke still billowed up, a dark smudge on the skyline.

"At least no one was killed," Cull said as the brothers stood shoulder to shoulder in the front yard. "I talked to Dad. His shoulder is better, but Abby called the doctor anyway."

"How long before we find out what caused it?" Boone asked.

"The fire chief said it should be a few days. Maybe a gas leak." Cull shook his head.

Ledger turned at the sound of a vehicle roaring up the road. "I'll be a son of a…" He stared in disbelief.

"Maybe you better let us handle this," Cull said, grabbing his arm as Ledger started toward the pickup that had just come to a dust-boiling stop in their yard.

He pulled his arm free. "Not a chance. I promised Abby I wouldn't go after him, but I told her all bets were off if he came out here." He stormed over to the pickup as Wade climbed out.

WADE DIDN'T NEED his father to tell him he was a damned fool for coming out here. But he had to know if Abby was all right. Now, though, as he saw the destroyed house, his heart lodged in his throat. If she was in that house when it exploded… His beautiful Abby.

He saw Ledger McGraw, the man he'd hated for years, stalking toward him. Abby had been in love with McGraw from the beginning. She would have married him if Wade's father and her mother hadn't lied to her. Wasn't that what had eaten him up inside for the past three years because he'd suspected it all along? He hadn't gotten Abby fair and square. She'd never wanted him. She'd always wanted McGraw.

He'd never felt such pain. And all of it had been for nothing. Especially if Abby was dead.

"Wade? What the hell are you doing here?" Ledger demanded as he advanced on him. The cowboy was covered with soot from fighting the fire and he looked angry enough to kill.

"Is Abby…?"

Ledger kept coming. Wade didn't even bother to throw up an arm as the cowboy punched him. He staggered under the blow but didn't go down. His father had hit him a lot harder than that in his life.

"Just tell me she's alive."

Ledger hit him again, this time driving him back before tackling him to the ground. Wade took another blow before his survival instincts cut in and he started to fight back. This man had been his nemesis for years. He hated him. Hated that Abby loved this man more than him.

But still McGraw was winning this battle.

"That's enough," a male voice ordered as Ledger was pulled off him.

Wade looked from Ledger to his brother Cull. Behind him was the older brother Boone.

"I would have let him beat the hell out of him a little longer, if it had been me," Boone said. All three of them looked like they wanted to kick his ass. He couldn't really blame them.

He wiped the blood from his cut lip with the back of his hand as he sat up. "Abby?"

"She's alive," Ledger said, glaring down at him. "No thanks to you."

Wade covered his face with his hands and, unable to hold back the burst of emotion, began to sob in relief and regret.

Chapter Eighteen

"You want the good news first?" Cull asked. They had all gathered in Cull's cabin, the largest one on the ranch now that the house was gone.

"Huck and Wade have been arrested." He looked at Abby, who was sitting next to Ledger on the couch. "They've both been charged, along with a tech at the lab and our cook. Huck and Wade won't be seeing daylight for many years to come. Vance is going to live—and turned state's evidence against them. He'll get some time, as well, but nothing like he should for his part of the charade."

Ledger saw his father nod solemnly. "I feel sorry for him. I saw something in him…" He shook his head. "I have more good news. While the house is a total loss, insurance will cover rebuilding. I actually think it's a good thing," he said, no doubt seeing that his sons were afraid he was taking it hard.

"It's a new beginning. Let's face it, there was a lot of sadness associated with that house."

"It was haunted," Cull said. Ledger knew he was only partially kidding.

His father nodded. "I suppose it was. But my life has changed since I built that house for your mother and our future."

Boone had been looking at his phone. He glanced up suddenly, shock on his face. "Jim Waters has been arrested trying to leave the country with a briefcase full of money." His gaze shot to their father. "Do you know anything about that?"

Travers's smile was almost sad. "Human nature. Jim apparently couldn't overcome his. It's probably just as well since Patricia's trial is coming up. She has implicated him in my poisoning."

Boone swore. "That son of—"

"I have some good news," Ledger interjected. "Wade has agreed to sign the divorce papers when the six months is up. He isn't going to contest it. Also he'll be going to prison and locked up for some time to come."

Travers reached over to squeeze his son's shoulder. "I'm happy for you. I suppose you'll want to start building a house for the two of you on the ranch. Looks like there'll be a lot of construction going on. I like that. I like progress."

"Me too," Ledger said and smiled over at Abby.

"Well," Cull said. "Nikki is going to be back this week. I hate to let my little brother beat me at anything…" He grinned. "I've asked Nikki to marry me. She's said yes!"

There was cheering. Travers suggested a toast.

"There's one more thing," Boone said. "Do you still want me to follow up on that last lead we had about Jesse Rose?"

"I do. But Vance taught me something," their father said. "I need to be more careful. If you don't mind checking it out…"

"Don't worry. If it's not legit, I'll know. Just don't get your hopes up."

"No," Travers said. "I'm going to drive down to the Crandall place. I need to talk to Tough."

"Dad—"

"Cull, I heard him just fine. He isn't interested in being a McGraw. I can live with that. But I believe he's my son. I can hope for some sort of relationship, can't I?"

LEDGER FOUND ABBY standing outside on the cabin porch, looking out at the ranch in the distance. For so long, smoke had curled up from the ruins of the house he almost thought he could still see. He would be glad when the debris was gone and the new house started.

Mostly, he wanted a fresh start with Abby. She'd been through so much. All he wanted to do was make her happy. He knew it couldn't be easy for her hearing about her soon-to-be ex-husband's arrest.

"Are you all right?" he asked as he joined her at the porch railing.

"I've made so many mistakes. If I had just followed my heart…" Abby began to cry.

Ledger pulled her into his arms. "Abby, we've all made mistakes. The moment I heard you married Wade, I should have come to you then. Maybe we could have sorted things out and you could have gotten an annulment since your marriage was based on a lie."

She nodded against his chest. "I should have trusted in our love."

"That's all behind us. I will never give you any reason to doubt it ever again."

"Your home, your beautiful…" She was crying harder. "It's all my fault."

He held her at arm's length. "Abby, it's just a building. No one was hurt. Dad is excited about rebuilding. You heard him. That house had too many ghosts." He wiped a tear from her cheek with his thumb. "I'm just sorry for everything you've had to go through. But that, too, is behind us."

She nodded and gave him a smile through her tears. "I don't know what I would have done without you."

"You'll never have to find out. I love you."

"I love you. My heart would break when you came into the café—and when you didn't."

He smiled at this woman he'd almost lost for good as he got down on one knee.

Abby's eyes widened as he squeezed her hand and asked, "Abby, will you marry me sometime in the future when you're a free woman?"

ABBY LOOKED DOWN at this man she'd loved for so long. He'd hung in, determined to be there for her even when she'd tried so hard to push him away. If it hadn't been for him, she knew she would be dead.

"Yes!" she said, her voice breaking. She'd never thought she'd see this day. "Oh, Ledger."

She dropped to her knees in front of him, falling into his arms.

He laughed and held her. "Don't you want to see the ring?"

She shook her head. "You can put a piece of string around my finger, for all I care. It doesn't matter. All I care about is being with you always."

"I guess I'll have to take this back," he said after pulling them both to their feet and opening the little black velvet box.

Abby gasped as she looked down at the pear-shaped diamond glittering up at her. "It's beautiful!"

"Just like you." He slipped it on her finger and then met her gaze. "I can wait as long as it takes."

"You've proven that," she said with a laugh.

"You can have any kind of wedding you want."

"I would love to marry you right now, right on this porch with your family as witnesses, if I could."

"I'll call the preacher the moment you're free—if that's what you want," he said, only half joking. "But I think we should do it up proud instead. I want you to have a wedding that you'll always remember." He looked into her eyes. "Meanwhile, I'll start building our house on the ranch. I need you to make it a home. You've seen my cabin."

She smiled. "But I'd still like to keep working at the café—at least until the baby comes."

"The baby?"

"The one you and I are going to make tonight," she said.

"Oh, *that* baby." He kissed her, knowing that things were finally as they should be. Ledger and Abby. Their marriage would be stronger because of the rough road that had gotten them here. And they would get married right here on the ranch.

But tonight they would be together again. He put his arm around her as they went inside and up the stairs to their room.

"ARE YOU ALL RIGHT?" Ledger asked late that night when he found his father standing outside in the moonlight.

"I'm fine," Travers said, wrapping an arm around his son and pulling him over next to him for a moment. "I was just thinking about when your mother and I started this ranch. We had such dreams. I think that was the problem. We didn't want this much. It kind of snowballed as the ranch became so successful. We had no idea that our luck was about to change."

"You can't blame your good fortune on what happened," he said.

"Can't I? Your mother never wanted all of this."

He heard something in his father's voice that sent his pulse pounding. "The twins?"

His father had never looked so old as he did in the moonlight. "You boys were her pride and joy. She was happy with the way things were. I was the one who wanted to give her a girl." He shook his head. "It was all too much for her."

"I'm so sorry."

Travers smiled at him. "How are you, son? I feel as if I haven't paid enough attention to the children I didn't lose."

"We're all fine."

"Your brother Cull is in love. Boone, well, who knows if he will ever find anyone as contrary as he is." He smiled when he said it. "And you and Abby?"

"We're good. We got engaged tonight."

Sadness filled his father's eyes. "Years ago when you came to me—"

"You were right. I was too young to get married."

"But not too young to lose your heart."

"No," he agreed. "I gave it away. There was no getting it back." He smiled. "I've always loved Abby. Nothing changed even when she married Wade."

"Well, that is all behind you now."

"Yes. We all have a chance for a new beginning."

His father sighed. "Let's just hope Boone finds Jesse Rose. Even if it is to know that she's alive and happy. That will be enough."

Epilogue

The sun shone in a cloudless blue sky on Abby and Ledger's wedding day. Standing with her friends around her, Abby felt a shiver of excitement. This was how it was supposed to be, she thought, remembering her other wedding day.

It had been just the four of them, she and Wade, her mother and Huck. She'd worn a pink dress with navy flowers. It was one she'd had in her closet, one that Wade said he liked on her. Huck had gotten her a rose to hold as they drove to the judge's chambers to be married.

Afterward, she and Wade had gone back to the house he had bought. A honeymoon had been out of the question. "Honeymoons are for people with money to throw away since they have nothing to do with marriage," her mother had said.

Abby remembered crying herself to sleep that night after Wade had dropped off. He'd drunk too much champagne, some cheap bottles that Huck had opened on the way from the judge's chambers.

She pushed those memories away like a rainstorm moving on. The sun was out; her friends were all around her. She could feel their excitement.

"You are absolutely glowing," said Sarah, one of the young women she worked with at the café. "I always knew the two of you would get together. The way Ledger always looked at you when he came into the café, it was clear that he loved you."

"It's nice to have you back," another friend said. Abby hugged her. Wade had kept her from her friends, saying they would just put bad ideas into her head.

Ella stuck her head in the door. "You ready?" Her boss looked beautiful in a red velvet dress. It was the first time Abby had seen her in anything other than a white uniform. She'd asked Ella to give her away.

"I'm not even going to ask about your mother," Ella had said. "I'd love to give you away."

Now Abby looked down at the bouquet in her hands. She lifted the flowers and sniffed the tiny white roses. Was this really happening?

She looked up. From the huge terrace behind the new house Travers had built, she could see the Little Rockies in the distance. Horses ran across open foothills, their manes blowing behind them. The day couldn't have been more perfect.

She'd always thought of this ranch as paradise. The times she'd spent here before Ledger went away to college and she married Wade were something she'd hung on to for the past few years.

Now she looked out over the ranch realizing that in a few minutes she would be Mrs. Ledger McGraw. It felt like a fantasy, something she hadn't dared let herself believe was possible.

She thought of Ledger. He'd never lost faith. She felt tears burn her eyes.

"Can you ever forgive me?" she'd asked him that night after they'd made love.

"There is nothing to forgive, Abby. You didn't burn down the house."

"No, Wade and his father did because of me."

"Honey," he'd said, pulling her to him. "Huck Pierce has had it in for my father since they were boys. This has nothing to do with you."

"But I believed their lies. I didn't trust you and I should have."

"Oh, Abby, I knew you'd been lied to but there was nothing I could do. If I'd had my way, I would have ridden into the café and swept you up on my horse and rode out of town with you."

She smiled through her tears. "I dreamed of you doing that."

He laughed. "So did I. But I couldn't. Not until I

knew you were ready to leave him. It was the hardest thing I'd ever done, waiting. But now there is nothing keeping us apart. The past is just that." He'd kissed her with such passion she'd let go of the guilt, the grief, the feeling that she could never be happy again.

With Ledger McGraw she could finally know passion, love, tenderness, and happiness.

"I'm ready," she said to Ella. "I've never been more ready."

LEDGER LOOKED UP and saw Abby as the wedding march played. She stepped out in a shaft of sunlight. She wore a string of daisies in her long hair. The dress was a pale yellow that flowed as she moved. She had never looked more beautiful.

His heart soared, making him have trouble catching his breath. He'd dreamed of this day for so long. Now it was finally happening.

"You going to be all right?" his father asked, standing next to him with Cull and Boone.

"I am now," he said.

"Didn't you ever want to give up?" Cull had asked him last night after everyone else had gone to bed. "I think I would have given up."

"You wouldn't have if it had been Nikki. Once you fall in love...nothing can change that."

"I'm happy for you, Ledger," Cull had said and

slapped him on the back. "Hope you're as happy as Nikki and I are being married."

"We will be."

As he watched his soon-to-be wife walk toward him, she smiled and their gazes met. He smiled back at her. The future couldn't have looked any brighter on this beautiful Montana summer day. Some things, he thought, were definitely worth waiting for.

* * * * *

INTRIGUE

Available September 19, 2017

#1737 ROUGH RIDER
Whitehorse, Montana: The McGraw Kidnapping
by B.J. Daniels
Boone McGraw is in Butte on the hunt for his kidnapped baby sister. What he wasn't expecting to find was private investigator C.J. Knight...and a whole lot of trouble.

#1738 PINE LAKE
by Amanda Stevens
Olive Belmont's sleepwalking condition has placed her at the scene of a crime and in the crosshairs of a vicious killer, and the only man who can save her is Jack King, who was once accused of a brutal murder himself...

#1739 POINT BLANK SEAL
Red, White and Built • by Carol Ericson
Navy SEAL sniper Miguel Estrada has endured a year of captivity and torture, but after breaking free and discovering his fiancée and their infant son are being followed, the nightmare may just be beginning.

#1740 TEXAS SHOWDOWN
Cattlemen Crime Club • by Barb Han
FBI agent Maria Belasco has lost all recent memories in an attack—forgetting that her husband, Austin O'Brien, was about to become her ex-husband. Can Austin help her recover her memory, even if it means the end for them all over again?

#1741 MR. SERIOUS
Mystery Christmas • by Danica Winters
Military police officer Waylon Fitzgerald left Mystery, Montana, behind to seek a life of adventure, which comes to a crashing halt when his ex-wife is accused of murder and goes on the run. But when he returns to the family ranch, there's more than a murder investigation waiting for him—a daughter he never knew he had.

#1742 STONE COLD CHRISTMAS RANGER
by Nicole Helm
Alyssa Jimenez is a bounty hunter with ties to the underworld that have taught her one thing—trust no one. But she has no choice but to rely on the protection of Texas Ranger Bennet Stevens during a risky investigation, and it's not just the case getting under her skin.

YOU CAN FIND MORE INFORMATION ON UPCOMING HARLEQUIN® TITLES,
FREE EXCERPTS AND MORE AT WWW.HARLEQUIN.COM.

HICNM0917

Get 2 Free Books,
Plus 2 Free Gifts—

just for trying the Reader Service!

HI17R

Detective Bobbie Gentry and serial-killer hunter Nick Shade's fates have been entwined since their first case—only together can they bring down the new menace to Savannah's elite and survive.

Read on for a sneak preview of
THE COLDEST FEAR,
the next installment in the **SHADES OF DEATH** *series from* USA TODAY *bestseller author* **Debra Webb**.

The simple definition of *fear* according to Merriam-Webster: "an unpleasant emotion caused by being aware of danger; a feeling of being afraid." Bobbie Gentry hadn't felt that emotion for her personal safety in 309 days.

As a detective with the Montgomery Police Department she encountered plenty of opportunities to fear for her well-being. Cops felt the cold, hard edge of fear on a daily basis. But it was difficult to fear death when all that mattered most in life was gone and the small steps she had dared take toward building a new one had been derailed.

A psychopathic serial killer known as the Storyteller had murdered her husband and caused the deaths of her child and the partner she loved like a father. Nearly a year later she had learned to some degree to live with the unthinkable reality and, wouldn't you know, along came another crushing blow. A second serial killer had devastated her life all over again. A fellow cop she'd dared to keep close had been brutally murdered a mere two days ago. His killer had left a message for her: "This one's just for you, Bobbie." The same killer had almost succeeded in taking the life of her uncle, the chief of police.

Bobbie sucked in a deep breath. How did she muster the strength to keep going? Revenge? Justice? She'd gotten both. The world was free of two more heinous killers and still it wasn't enough. The expected relief and satisfaction came, but the hollow feeling, the emptiness, remained her constant companion. *But* there was the tiniest glimmer of hope. A fragile bond had formed between her and the man who'd helped her stop the two monsters who had destroyed so many lives, including hers. The development was completely unexpected, but surprisingly not unwelcome.

Nick Shade had given her something she'd been certain she would never again feel: the desire to live for more than revenge…for more than merely clipping on her badge each morning. Now he needed her help—whether he would admit as much or not.

Those who knew of his existence called him the serial-killer hunter. Nick was unlike any man Bobbie had known. Brooding, intense, impossible to read and yet deeply caring and self-sacrificing. At twenty-one he had discovered his father, Randolph Weller, was a depraved serial killer with forty-two murders to his credit. Since ensuring his father was brought to justice, Nick had dedicated his life to finding and stopping the vicious serial killers no one else seemed able to catch. Like Bobbie, he'd stopped feeling much of anything beyond that driving need for justice a very long time ago. Maybe that was the bond that had initially connected them—the thin, brittle ties of utter desolation and desperation. Two broken people urgently attempting to make a difference that neither of them could completely define nor hope to quantify.

Yet they'd found something together. Something that felt real.

Don't miss
THE COLDEST FEAR,
available September 2017 wherever
MIRA® Books and ebooks are sold.

www.Harlequin.com

Need an adrenaline rush from nail-biting tales
(and irresistible males)?

Check out **Harlequin® Intrigue®**
and **Harlequin® Romantic Suspense** books!

New books available every month!

CONNECT WITH US AT:

Harlequin.com/Community

 Facebook.com/HarlequinBooks

 Twitter.com/HarlequinBooks

 Instagram.com/HarlequinBooks

 Pinterest.com/HarlequinBooks

ReaderService.com

**ROMANCE WHEN
YOU NEED IT**

LOVE
Harlequin
romance?

Join our Harlequin community to share your thoughts and connect with other romance readers!

Be the first to find out about promotions, news, and exclusive content!

Sign up for the Harlequin e-newsletter and download a free book from any series at

www.TryHarlequin.com

CONNECT WITH US AT:

Harlequin.com/Community

 Facebook.com/HarlequinBooks

 Twitter.com/HarlequinBooks

 Instagram.com/HarlequinBooks

 Pinterest.com/HarlequinBooks

ReaderService.com

**ROMANCE WHEN
YOU NEED IT**

HSOCIAL2017

THE WORLD IS BETTER
WITH
Romance

Harlequin has everything from contemporary, passionate and heartwarming to suspenseful and inspirational stories.

Whatever your mood,
we have a romance just for you!

Connect with us to find your next great read,
special offers and more.

f /HarlequinBooks

🐦 @HarlequinBooks

www.HarlequinBlog.com

www.Harlequin.com/Newsletters

H HARLEQUIN®

A *Romance* FOR EVERY MOOD™

www.Harlequin.com

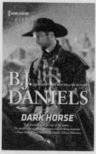

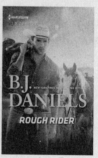